CW00823510

THE
RELUCTANT
WARRIOR

THE
RELUCTANT
WARRIOR

AN AMERICAN AIRMAN'S STORY

Barry RICKSON

authorHOUSE®

AuthorHouse™ UK Ltd.
1663 Liberty Drive
Bloomington, IN 47403 USA
www.authorhouse.co.uk
Phone: 0800.197.4150

© 2013 by Barry RICKSON. All rights reserved.

No part of this book may be reproduced, stored in a retrieval system, or
transmitted by any means without the written permission of the author.

Published by AuthorHouse   10/17/2013

ISBN: 978-1-4918-8153-8 (sc)
ISBN: 978-1-4918-8154-5 (e)

Any people depicted in stock imagery provided by Thinkstock are models,
and such images are being used for illustrative purposes only.
Certain stock imagery © Thinkstock.

This book is printed on acid-free paper.

Because of the dynamic nature of the Internet, any web
addresses or links contained in this book may have changed
since publication and may no longer be valid. The views
expressed in this work are solely those of the author and do
not necessarily reflect the views of the publisher, and the
publisher hereby disclaims any responsibility for them.

CONTENTS

1

ARRIVAL IN BREMEN, JANUARY 1939

The young man felt distinctly uneasy as he stepped off the train. He was Frank Eberhardt, a good-looking, blond 20 year-old American of German ancestry who was arriving at Bremen Hauptbahnhof in northern Germany in January 1939. Frank was a native of Wilkes Barre, Pennsylvania, and had been sent by his father, a middle manager at a New York branch of the German chemical giant IG Farben, to study their business methods at first-hand and to improve his knowledge of the language. He was a college student at the University of Pennsylvania where he shone at football, probably more so than in the lecture room. This was a highly prestigious university, founded by the great Benjamin Franklin, and Frank's family were so proud that he had been admitted there as a student.

He and his father had decided it would be better if he were to take a year off from his academic studies and go to Germany to gain experience. He could then graduate and return for a junior position with IGF with the potential for a position in lower management. The university's business school had a fine reputation throughout the country and was certainly providing him with an unrivalled learning experience. Although not outstandingly academic, Frank was certainly intelligent, had common sense and good social skills. Because he was handsome, he was a little vain. He occasionally had been known to lose his temper, but was usually good-natured. In his teens he had had a few, shall we say, differences of opinion with his parents about his lifestyle, such as coming in late, not working hard enough at college or mixing with people with whom they did not approve. Occasionally, these rows had finished up in his slamming the door and disappearing upstairs. With growing maturity, however, he was beginning to realise that his parents had usually been right. There was still a difference between them politically as his father being conservative in all ways voted Republican, whereas the more liberal-minded Frank, as perhaps reaction against his father, was a supporter of the Democrats. His mother who professed no interest in politics took neither side in their discussions.

Even if the United States were several thousand miles away from Europe, they were aware of the worsening situation there. Their president, Franklin D Roosevelt, had promised the people that they would not be drawn into any conflict and that they would remain neutral. Frank, at heart a pacifist, was uneasy about the American connection with IG Farben which, under the guidance of Hermann Schmidt, had been assisted by Wall Street financiers into making it so absolutely essential to the military power of Adolf Hitler.

Frank had gone by sea from New York to the Hook of Holland. He had enjoyed the sea trip as the Atlantic had been quite calm considering the time of year and he liked talking to some of the other passengers, especially younger females. What had surprised him was the number of Germans on the boat. Why were so many making the homeward trip? "Circumstances," was the usual enigmatic response.

Once in harbour, he had to wait for three hours for the train. During this wait when speaking to various people, he had begun to realise just what these circumstances could be. It was obvious that the Dutch people were suspicious of Germany's intentions even though they had managed to stay out of The Great War. The train journey across Holland took him through Rotterdam and Arnhem. He hadn't realised just how flat and low-lying the country was and he was very surprised at the number of windmills. It struck him as being a very peaceful country and he had conversations with several Dutch people who were very curious as to why an American would be travelling to Germany.

As well as being impressed by their friendliness, he was also surprised at how many could speak good English. Many left the train before crossing the German frontier, leaving Frank to try his uncertain German with the remaining passengers; however, his attention was soon taken with other things.

After the train had crossed the frontier into Germany, he was all too aware of the country's embrace of the Third Reich with large Nazi red, white and black standards with the swastika at every station and in the towns and villages en route. From what he could understand listening to the conversations he heard on the train, there seemed to be great enthusiasm for the Führer and his policies which had brought so much prosperity after the grim years of the 1920s and early 30s. The re-taking of the Rhineland and takeover of Czechoslovakia were seen as great triumphs and proofs of the Fatherland's re-emergence as a world power. Adolf Hitler had carried out his pledge of giving the German people more Lebensraum, or living space. There was growing evidence of Germany's militaristic aims as troops of the Wehrmacht and tanks were to be seen along the route and army uniforms were everywhere on the train. He had seen films and read magazines about the Nazi Party rallies at Nuremburg; these he had found spectacular and colourful, yet rather terrifying in their fanaticism and intense dedication to Hitler. "Don't worry," his father had said, "We are neutrals and thousands of miles away from it all."

Not only did Frank feel rather ill-at-ease in what seemed a very alien environment, but he knew he was going to miss his friends, male and female, especially the latter. He had no special girl-friend but was quite fond of Carmel, a pretty, dark-haired girl who had Spanish blood in her veins. She was still a student at Frank's college where she was reading modern languages. He had lost his virginity to her in a rather hurried, fumbling and not too satisfying encounter, after a ball at college. They were still good friends and she had been sorry to see him leave. There had been quite a tearful farewell as they said goodbye when Frank embarked at New York for the cross-Atlantic trip to Europe. Frank promised to write to her regularly.

He steps into a taxi outside the station and asks in reasonable German to be taken to his lodgings in Bismarck Strasse, close to the River Weser which he remembered from reading, or being made to read, Robert Browning's "Pied Piper of Hamelin." Accommodation had been arranged for him here by his father's super-efficient secretary liaising with the

Bremen branch. On the way there he is depressed even more when he sees many young men in Hitler Youth uniforms behaving so arrogantly strutting round the streets with groups of them in the town hall square. Many seem to be harassing an old man and mocking him, a Star of David conspicuous on his sleeve.

On arrival at his lodgings he is greeted quite warmly by his landlady, Frau Winifred Lütze, and shown to his room, which is fairly small but seemed comfortable enough. He guesses that Frau Lütze is in her late forties. She is elegant, has slightly greying hair, blue eyes and a welcoming smile. She tells him that she had been made a widow in 1916 when her husband had been killed on the Somme. She missed Karl dreadfully but shows no bitterness towards Frank; in fact she is pleased with the extra income as her pension is only just adequate. Her two sons had been conscripted into the army in 1938 and are doing their basic training, Nils in Bavaria and Gerd near Kassel. Their photographs, together with her late husband's, all in army uniform, are displayed prominently on the wall.

She allows him to settle into his room and unpack before inviting him downstairs for Kaffee und Kuchen and to give them both a chance to get to know each other. There is a comfortable looking bed with a thick, soft eiderdown, which looks very inviting after his long journey. The wardrobe and chest of drawers would be adequate for the amount of clothes he has brought with him. Everything is very clean and tidy and he guesses that the room had belonged to one of her sons as the colour scheme is very plain and not a bit "girly."

Later she gives him a very welcome German-type meal of Bratwurst and Spargel, a type of asparagus. He will sample many types of Wurst during his stay in Bremen. For dessert he is given Phannkuchen, a delicious type of pancake. He will soon find that Frau Lütze is an excellent cook, something which allays his mother's fears about how her boy is going to manage. He is amazed at the different types of bread that can be had, at least ten. He loves to sample various ones at breakfast with ham, salami and all kinds of cheeses. The coffee is very strong which suits him.

2

SETTLING IN

Two days later he reports to the offices of the company where he is made to feel welcome by Gerhardt Ecke, his section head, a very smartly dressed man of about forty with a centre parting in his black hair. A tour of the factory follows which makes a great impression upon him as everything is so immaculate and the workforce is so focussed. Introductions are made to those who will be his immediate colleagues and already he feels that his rusty German is improving, at least in understanding.

He writes home to his parents to say that he has arrived safely, has comfortable accommodation and that he is getting on quite well at work. These of course are just the sort of reassuring words that his mother wants to hear, whereas his father would have liked a little more about his work. As the days go by he finds that most of his workmates are friendly enough, but before long they notice his little weakness, his vanity. As one of them says," Der Amerikaner ist sehr eitel; er schaut sich immer im Spiegel an!" commenting on his love of the mirror. There remain some who seem rather suspicious. Why would a young American be sent all this way to work in a German firm of such renown and engaged in such obvious military activities? He is very young, but could this be clever subterfuge and a way of putting them off guard as to his undercover work? Just where does the United States stand in its view of Germany in any case? Although they have professed their neutrality, they are linked to England by a common language and seem to have close ties in many ways.

Frank doesn't understand everything but enough to realise this undercurrent, not of hostility exactly, but of wariness and scepticism. However, he is on the whole enjoying his experience and decides he must find out more of this city where he is to spend the next few months. He is impressed by some of its old buildings, especially the green-roofed St Petri Cathedral. He becomes a regular visitor to the excellent Bierkellers, especially the one under the Rathaus, or town hall. He soon finds that he is able to make friends with local young people who are fascinated with his American-accented German which is steadily improving. After seeing his own country dominated by Ford cars, he is surprised at the number of Volkswagens, the so-called People's Car, which has been in mass production under Hitler's orders.

Bremen, although some seventy miles from the sea, is a great thriving port and he loves to walk along the river bank seeing all the great ships coming and going, barges, merchant vessels, tugs, but he also notices many ships of the German Kriegsmarine, including submarines which he has discovered are built and repaired there. He mentions this one day at work and Klaus Merkel, a very keen National Socialist, is bursting with pride as he tells him how on May 4th 1935 (he knows the date precisely) the beloved Führer was on board the Scharnhorst on the River Weser. Launched in 1936 from Wilhelmshaven, close to Bremen, the very imposing battleship was a key weapon in the German navy's bid to rule the seas. There were thousands lining the banks, cheering and waving flags. Men and women of all ages were chanting Sieg Heil and singing the national anthem, "Deutschland über Alles", detachments of the Hitler Jugend were playing militaristic tunes, veterans of the First World War were proudly displaying their medals; all were overcome with national pride. All this seemed to

Franz to be approaching hysteria rather than healthy patriotism.

Klaus by now with tears in his eyes hadn't finished yet. Seeing his leader on the mighty battle cruiser had been the greatest experience of his life, but he also recalled previous visits to the city such as on December 14th 1934 — again the date was etched in his mind — when their leader made his fourth visit to the city, but the first as Chancellor. Klaus had been there too and was so enthusiastic in recalling the day. One of the other workers said quietly to Frank not to worry too much as they weren't all quite as "erregbar" or excitable as he was. The young American nodded in seeming assent but from what he had seen in his short time in Germany there were very many like Klaus. It was now March and he had the distinct feeling that war was in the air.

3

ROMANTIC MEETING

One of his favourite spots in the city was a little bar near the Hauptbahnhof called Haus Helgoland. He went there quite regularly with his colleagues Franz and Paul after work or on a Saturday evening. Franz is about the same age as Frank and supports the local soccer team Werder Bremen, but this is a game which Frank knows little about; however, Franz promises to take him there one day. Paul is a little older than Frank and has come up from Kassel to serve an apprenticeship. He has a good understanding of English and finds the books of Mark Twain extremely funny, as does Frank. He tries to think of any of his contemporaries at home who can read German literature, but cannot.

Early one cold Wednesday evening with snow lying thick on the pavements and after a hard day at work when he had had a little altercation with his section leader, he decided to go to Haus Helgoland alone. After some half-hour or so, a very pretty, dark-haired girl caught his attention. He couldn't stop looking at her and wanted to make some excuse to approach her, but what could he say? What could he do? Did Germans use the equivalent cliché, "Kommen Sie hier oft"? in such situations? If he did say this, would she laugh at his strange foreign accent, or even worse, just ignore him? She had several of her friends with her who were all talking excitedly and obviously enjoying themselves. They looked like a group of office workers probably thawing out and having a quick drink before going off home. They were all quite attractive, but she stood out. To meet her on her own would be well-nigh impossible. The worse deterrent of all, however, was that such a good-looking girl, slim, dark, with a very attractive figure would not be short of boy-friends; why should she be interested in such a gauche Auslander?

He had written regularly to his friends in America, including occasionally to Carmen, but he felt no real passion there now, just a good friendship. As is usually the case, if there were some girl who really appealed to him, he was too nervous to approach, whereas he had fewer inhibitions with those he would just look upon as good friends. He just could not summon up the courage to make any approach.

He was unable to get her out of his mind and thought about her when he should have been thinking about his work. Often his concentration would waver and once his section head reprimanded him, asking if he had been listening when some important instructions were being given. He had to do something about this; otherwise, he would go mad. Perhaps she would go again to the Haus Helgoland, and even if she had friends with her he would pluck up the courage to make some approach, whatever the pretext.

With this in mind, he decided that he should revisit the bar. He went several times in the hope of seeing her there, perhaps on her own. Why should a young girl want to go there alone? She could be calling in to kill time waiting for a train at the nearby station or waiting for a bus? She could have had a hard day at work and just wanted a little refreshment before returning home? By the way, where did she live and what work did she do, if any? All these questions were constantly in his mind.

He had come to the conclusion that it was not to be when one warm May evening after he had called in following a long day at work which began at seven, he could hardly believe that she was there sitting in a corner, by herself, moreover. Now what can he do! He appraises the situation, realising he has to make his move before she leaves. Fortunately there is a vacant table next to her, so that is a good start.

He sits down and notices with a sly glance that she seems to have only just started her glass of lager, so that is another stroke of luck. He starts to think over the advice of his father, something that was never lacking: "Son, if you want something badly enough, you must go for it." At the moment he can't think of something he wants more badly! He mumbles something about the recent good weather, always a good standby conversational opener. She smiles — oh, how encouraging! — before asking him if he has had a good day. He then asks her if he may sit at her table. "Natürlich," she replies. Frank is wondering if this is a dream which will come to an end when he wakes up.

Frank is beginning to become more relaxed as he orders another drink for the pair of them. She is called Helga and as she knows some English, they talk to each other in a mixture of English and German, the equivalent of Franglais. She finds his American accent "niedlich," which they work out means "cute." She is studying Law at Hamburg University and has also had a long day in the library in Bremen whilst on a short vacation. He looks at his watch and to his surprise sees it is almost nine o'clock, and he arrived there not long after six. As he is a gentleman, he asks if he may escort her home. She seems a little reluctant, but it turns out that this is because she lives about twelve kilometres away in a little town called Delmenhorst which Frank has never heard of. He has another early start the next day, but this is not going to put him off the chance of seeing more of Helga. They go to the station and catch the train to her home town where they arrive just after ten o'clock.

4

TOURING BREMEN
AND HAMBURG

He takes her home to the corner of the street where she lives which is just near the station. Helga asks him to go no further as her father is rather protective of her, especially where foreigners are concerned. However, is he brave enough to ask if he may meet her again? To his great relief she agrees to do so and a meeting is arranged for the following Saturday, at Haus Helgoland, of course.

As this was only Wednesday, the week dragged terribly and his concentration at work was not all it should have been.

"Frank, do you have those estimates I asked you for you the other day?

"I am so sorry, Herr Ecke, but I have not had the time with other projects as well."

"Herr Eberhardt, we have to work to close schedules in this firm. Do you understand?"

"I am so sorry; I will have them on your desk this evening."

The change from the friendly "Frank" to "Herr" made him realise just how much was expected when working for one of the top firms in the Reich; only just recently had he been addressed by his first name which was something of a breakthrough in a far more formal society than he was used to back at home. This minor reprimand was fully deserved he knew and he would have to focus more on his work than on Helga—far more easily said than done!

At last Saturday came and he met Helga at one o'clock as arranged. Actually, he had been looking in the window of a nearby shop for the last twenty minutes, having been fearful of being late and finding that she had gone.

She is there and they find a table before ordering two glasses of Beck's, the pride of the city's beer industry.

"Helga, I was so fearful that you would not come. You may have thought that I was too "vorwitzig", is it, or "cheeky" as we say?"

"Gar nicht, du bist nicht frech. Now, how would you like to see some of the interesting spots in our beautiful city?"

Frank readily agrees and is more and more impressed by her knowledge of English, which just adds to his feelings for her. She is unlike any other girl he has ever met. Does her foreign accent add to her attraction? Does his loneliness in this city so far away from home and her being so friendly make Helga more attractive than ever?

They start by going to the twin-towered St. Peter's Cathedral, St Petri Dom zu Bremen, with its picturesque green-leaded roof in the square close to Haus Helgoland, very near to the Rathaus, or town hall, also with its colourful green roof. There is the ancient Bierkeller below the Rathaus, which Helga slyly suggests Frank could want to visit soon. The statue of Roland in the square is also pointed out. She then takes him to the historic district of Schnoor which he finds so interesting.

Frank is given a history lesson as they move on. She tells him about the pride the citizens have in being an ancient member of the Hanseatic League, a kind of superior medieval trade union of great ports in northern Germany. The story of the great harbour she covers in a way that makes history far more interesting than it ever was at school or college when taught by middle-aged men.

Over the next few weeks as their friendship flourishes with visits to the parks and river trips, it is becoming clearer that this is the first serious relationship that each one has had. Frank had been

19

certain that such an attractive, intelligent girl must have other young men interested in her and dares to ask her the question. She is friendly with many boys she answers but with none seriously. "Sei nicht albern!" – "Don't be so silly!" By now they are holding hands like a committed couple and Frank will never forget their first kiss. It was as they stood on the corner of Helga's street as he had taken her home. It was so romantic as they held each other very tightly, locked in a firm embrace. "Oh God, please may his moment never end!" By this time all thoughts of Carmen have virtually disappeared, not that she has been sending too many letters.

One fine Tuesday in early July Helga suggests that they go to Hamburg for the day as Frank has a day off and her studies at university have been suspended for the summer. They make an early start by train on a journey he is looking forward to as he has heard so much of this great port. Helga has told him that it has some lovely buildings and parks. Just like Bremen she reminds him, it too is a member of the Hanseatic League and is very proud of its status. She is enjoying her time there after her first year.

When they get off the train, there are the red, black and white swastika flags everywhere on the station and in the streets outside. Uniforms of all branches of the armed forces, including the dreaded SS and Gestapo, are almost more visible than people in civilian dress. This is a city that seems more at war than Bremen. Helga takes him to the centre of the city where he sees the beautiful city hall, its superb architecture spoiled by the inevitable Nazi flags and banners all over the building. They go for a walk in the nearby Botanical Gardens. Close to them is the Binnenalster and just across the road is the much bigger Aussenalster. Helga explains that these are two artificial lakes made by damming the River Alster. There is much of interest on these two lakes, especially with all the pleasure boats and other craft to be seen. How lovely to see these scenes of peace in the middle of so much aggression.

There is a very impressive building on the side of the Aussenalster which attracts Frank's interest. Helga tells him that it is a hotel only for the rich and famous and is called Hotel Atlantic Kempinski. It is a place where wealthy visitors from the United States on trans-Atlantic liner trips would stay. Frank is eager to see it at closer quarters. He is suitably impressed when he does so for it is a magnificent-looking hotel with every appearance of luxury. They look at the mouth-watering menu on the door at a price far above their means. Helga teases him by saying that one day if he is a good boy, she could take him there for Nachmittags Tee. The promise of afternoon tea in this symbol of luxury is something to aim for, so he will be on his best behaviour from now on, he assures her.

Before having a meal, they take a look at the busy harbour area on the River Elbe. If Bremen seems on a war footing, this is nothing as compared with what they see now. There are the giant Blöhm and Voss shipyards with warships under construction, U-Boats waiting to go for sea-trials, smaller ships with their grey war-paint and a host of smaller craft scurrying to and fro like busy ants.

They then go for a meal which Helga recommends as being typical for Hamburg. Unfortunately there are rather too many loud sailors from the docks and not a few noisy party members. However, they decide to go ahead and order. The main course Is Birnen, Bohnen und Speck, a dish of green beans, pears and bacon. For dessert they have Franzbrötchen, a kind of croissant with raisins and cinnamon which they find delicious. They leave fairly quickly after they have eaten, especially after one of the sailors, who is rather drunk, starts to make inappropriate remarks to Helga. In spite of the overall atmosphere of war and the incident with the drunken sailor, they have enjoyed their day there and both would love to go there again in happier times. The food was excellent, some of the sights were very memorable and above all they had each other for company.

Although he is so happy in her company, he is growing more and more concerned with the increasingly aggressive attitudes he sees all around him. Uniforms are everywhere, there is an air of not very pleasant self-confidence, the huge red and white flags and banners with the black swastika emblem are in profusion, covering even religious buildings such as the cathedral. Loud noises are being made about increasing Lebensraum and can the indignities of Versailles be ended? This seems to be a country on the verge of war. What a background to this burgeoning romance!

Frank has tried very hard not to broach the subject of politics with her, but he does know, however, that she is uneasy about the way her country is going, especially as one of her best friends has Jewish blood. She has occasionally let slip some derogatory remark about some of the louts going round intimidating any they see as inferior, or those who are slow in returning their Nazi salute.

It is now the end of July and Helga thinks it could be time to meet her family. Frank is very nervous at the thought as he is not sure how they will take to him, an English speaker and native of the USA; she has assured him that her parents are not fervent Nazis, although her 15 year-old brother Karl is a keen member of the Hitler Youth.

5

MEET THE FAMILY

On a Saturday afternoon in early July Helga meets Frank at Delmenhorst station from where they take the short walk to her home. It is a very simple but comfortable house with a great orderliness about it. There are several ornaments in the Wohnzimmer, the main room, including what seem to be many family heirlooms. Herr Wassermann is a foreman in the docks, so there are many prints and paintings of ships from medieval times to the modern period. Frank also notices a wall plaque with the inscription of Bremen—Hansebund. As Helga had previously told Frank, her family were all proud to be Hanseaten, a privilege shared with citizens of Hamburg and other leading north German ports.

The greeting from Helga's parents is formal, but not too unwelcoming. Herr Wassermann is very well-built with a muscular body. He has dark hair, brown eyes, a deep scar on his left cheek and walks with a slight limp. He understands English quite well which he has picked up from working in the docks and meeting English and American sailors. Frau Wasserman's knowledge is not quite as good, but she is not completely lost. She is petite, has blue eyes and is rather attractive in a quiet kind of way. Frank's German has obviously improved enormously and consequently the conversation is going well after an initial nervousness on both sides. Frank is addressed as Herr Eberhardt by both parents as he is quizzed about his feelings on coming to Germany, his impressions of what he has seen, his life in the USA, his future on returning home etc., etc. Politics are kept very much in the background. Frau Wassermann becomes more and more hospitable— he is a handsome young man after all!

Half an hour or so later, Helga's 15 year-old brother, a blond blue-eyed boy with a good physique, comes in wearing a Hitler Youth uniform. He gives a cursory "Guten Tag" to Frank before launching into an enthusiastic description of the meeting he had just been to. From what he understands Frank is rather disturbed at realising just how brainwashed he is as he is so excited at the talk he has heard from their district leader. He has been emphasising what a superior race the Aryans are and how Germany is meant to dominate Europe and put those Jews and Slavs in their place. It becomes more and more frightening as he continues, until his father puts up his hand and orders him to stop as they have a visitor. Helga seems embarrassed and feels, but does not exactly say, that her father has been too tolerant in letting him carry on as he has.

After a very appetising meal of Bratkartoffeln and Wienerschnitzel with the inevitable and welcome Beck's beer, Frank decides he had better not outstay his welcome and takes his leave of the Wassermann family after thanking them for their hospitality. Herr Wassermann even hints that they perhaps could meet again soon and young Karl tries his best to say goodbye in English: "Very please to met you, Herr Eberhardt." Helga offers to escort him to the station. On the way Frank asks her about her father's injured cheek and his limp. She says that he is very lucky to be alive as in the Great War near Messines Ridge he was hit by a piece of shrapnel in the cheek. On the way to the hospital the ambulance went over a mine which fractured his leg. Frank is sympathetic and prays that there will never be another war of such devastation. When the United States entered the war in 1917, his uncle was sent to France and was slightly injured in the Argonne Forest.

On the way there Frank tells her that her family have been so "Gemütlich" to him and he is so grateful.

"I think they like you, but young Karl is perhaps a little suspicious as you didn't seem too happy when he was telling you about his meetings with the youth group. Did you know that next month they are going for three days into the Harz Mountains on a leadership course? He will be so proud if he passes — but I shall still have my Vorbehalten — do you say "reservations?" She has to admit that she is a member of the Hitler Youth equivalent for girls Bund Deutscher Mädel, not through choice but for girls 14-18 it is more or less compulsory. She then gives a sly smile as she says that Mutti thought he was handsome and this was making her jealous! He asks Helga to tell him her parents' Christian names, as in the rather formal German society they have not told him. Klaus and Margrit is the answer.

They continue to meet, either in Bremen or Delmenhorst, but they don't overdo going to her home. Helga tells Frank about the history of this quiet little town. It had been occupied in 1806 by a French and Dutch army and had been part of Napoleon's empire from 1811 to 1813. What a combination of brains and beauty she is and he asks her if she has ever thought of becoming a travel guide in her spare time.

"Das ist keine schlechte Idee, aber ich glaube nicht. I have too much work to do at university."

One thing that has struck Frank so much in his visits to Delmenhorst has been the ever-present, but not unpleasant, smell of the lino factory which provides much of the town's economy and gives so much employment. The memory of this is something that he will carry with him for the rest of his days. There is also the water tower which they seem quite fond of and this also will remain etched in his memory.

Much of their conversation continued to be conducted in this manner in a combination of English and German, with Helga being a little more adept bilingually but Frank was improving in this way as his confidence grew. He was becoming used to the differing accents of his work colleagues and he was able to discern the verbal traps they were setting him as they tried to embarrass him with low-level language and slang expressions. One of the office girls gave him a little present of a small beer mug after he had helped her with a short English lesson. He thanked her in German for this "gift" and wondered why everybody found this so funny. It was pointed out to him eventually that that meant "poison "in German; he should have said "Geschenk."

He was also learning much about the business of producing lubricating oil, synthetic rubber and aviation fuel manufactured by the very powerful IG Farben company. He was concerned, however, by how much of this was so obviously going into war production.

One evening when Frau Lütze has gone for the weekend to see her son in Kassel, Frank asks Helga to come into his lodgings. She is a little reluctant at first for, after all, she is a well brought-up girl with a fairly strict father. All he is asking is for her to see what his accommodation is like and have a coffee before catching the train back to Delmenhorst. But before long Frank suggests that Helga leaves her comfortable armchair to join him on the settee as he has something to show her in the local paper that he is looking at with pictures of a Hitler Youth rally in nearby Ganderksee. Perhaps her brother is on them? Before not too long they lose interest in the photos and hold hands tightly. He puts his arms round her and they start to kiss passionately and one thing leads to another. He starts to kiss her on the neck, then he undoes the buttons on her blouse before touching her well-rounded breasts. He takes off her blouse, then slides off her bra before putting his lips on her bosom. She helps him to undress her and he caresses her inner thighs. Can he really be about to make love to this beautiful girl that he was initially so shy of approaching all that time ago in Haus Helgoland? This can't be true — is he dreaming? She asks him to be careful as she is a Jungfrau and he seems to have more experience than her. They are both so carried away in their ecstasy, "Wie wunderbar! Oh Gott, ich liebe dich so viel!" Frank tells her that has been the most wonderful experience of his life; all of his other experiences have been as nothing.

As she starts to dress, she confesses to a sense of guilt because she has not known him very long and she has lost her virginity to this comparative stranger. There is no guilt in true love; he tells her that it is love, not lust, that is the cause of their relationship. Helga readily agrees before reminding Frank that she will miss the train if she doesn't hurry. After more ardent kissing at the station watched by some older passengers who look on with a mixture of amusement and disapproval, Helga leaves and they arrange their next meeting.

This increased intimacy has led Frank to becoming jealous. One evening as he is strolling past Haus Helgoland on his way to the station he sees her with a young man at a table in the corner. She is smiling and talking to him in a way that makes him think that they are on very friendly terms. He doesn't go in but carries on to the station feeling very upset. How well does she know this man? What were they talking about? He cannot settle until he finds out the truth. He finds it difficult to concentrate at work next day wondering who he is and how well she knows him. He has one consolation he tells himself; he is more handsome than this rival.

When he meets Helga the following day, she asks him why he has such a long face. He tells her that he is very upset about what he saw two days ago. When he tells her emotionally and tearfully the reason for his being so crestfallen, she is so disappointed with him at this outpouring of jealousy and this lack of trust in her. This rival "lover" was in fact her cousin from Hamburg who had been to Bremen on business and had contacted her at her home when they had arranged to have a quick meeting. She becomes angry and asks since when was one banned from meeting close relatives. Should they carry on their relationship? Frank is so upset at how foolish he has been and begs her forgiveness. She was a little slow in accepting his apologies, but gradually relented. "Du Dummkopf!" — "You silly child!" They then kissed and made up.

However, events are unfolding rapidly outside the lives of these two lovers and war seems to be drawing ever closer. It is impossible to go into Bremen without seeing more and more soldiers and members of the Kriegsmarine in the streets and even such a backwater as Delmenhorst is a home to military barracks opposite the main hospital. With such fervour and aggressive optimism in the air it seems only a matter of time before war breaks out.

On September 1st, 1939, the German radio announces that in response to border atrocities by the Poles, the German government has had no alternative but to invade Poland. Broadcasts are made by the Führer and by the Minister of Propaganda, Josef Goebbels, denouncing the treachery of Poland as troops pour over the border and the Luftwaffe attacks cities and military formations. Two days later Britain and France declare war on Germany. Where does this leave Frank?

His father had been pressing for him to return home for several weeks and now he sends him an urgent telegram: although the United States are not at war, they do have strong ties with Britain and it could be difficult for Frank to stay.

6

U.S.A. 1939

There seems no alternative as he says farewell to his workmates and, of course, to Helga. Many of his colleagues are disappointed to see him go as he has won them over with his friendly disposition and his growing mastery of the language, in all its levels! He has even admitted to Franz after having seen Werder Bremen play some team from München that the game had its points, but was inferior to the American brand. Others of his acquaintances have hinted at his being almost a coward in running off at the moment of Germany assuming its greatness.

The biggest difficulty for him has naturally been saying farewell to his girlfriend. The goodbye at the boat terminal in Bremen is long and tearful as they swear undying love. He had come to Germany without any romantic attachment and he was now leaving deeply in love. Helga for her part was in exactly the same situation: before meeting Frank she was friends with several boys, but not with anyone in particular. This had now changed and she was in love with this young man who was having to travel home several thousands of miles away. Would it ever be possible that they could meet again?

The ship crossing the Atlantic is full to capacity with passengers escaping from the European war, a high proportion of those being Jewish people who have been able to leave in one way or another. The news coming through from Britain is relayed incessantly with increasingly glum news concerning Poland. In London especially, the details are given of blackout precautions as heavy Luftwaffe air raids are expected from the first day. For many passengers the mood on board ship is sombre and downbeat as people move around with little animation, especially those who have left loved ones behind; but on the other hand for many there is a great feeling of relief to have got away.

For Frank there is only one thought on his mind: Helga. Will she still be thinking of him? What is she going to do now? Will she be allowed to continue her studies, or will she be diverted to help in the war effort?

He has many conversations with his fellow passengers, many of whom have extraordinary stories to tell of their experiences in managing to leave just in time. There was Jacob Arnstein who had been arrested for protesting on the evening of Kristallnacht when the synagogue had been burned down in Berlin's Orianenburg Strasse. He had been roughly treated by the police, thrown into a cell and then sent to a detention centre. He had escaped in a refuse cart, managed to make his way to Hamburg, and assumed another identity. Frank had long discussions with Dr. Bohle, a one-time physics lecturer at Leipzig University, who had taken the opportunity to flee the Nazi oppression. He told how the state's anti-semitic policy had become more and more intolerable and thousands of Jews had taken the opportunity to leave the country of their birth.

Frank had been aware of the way in which even the most qualified of men had been barred from carrying on in their profession and had to take menial jobs whilst being forced to wear the humiliating Star of David. He had known little of the true extent of the Nuremburg Laws of 1935 which took away the right of citizenship for Jewish people, nor of just to what extent their property and goods had been seized. He was told how for the Berlin Olympics there had been apparently some relaxation of the restrictions so as to escape the possibility of the Games being taken elsewhere ; Germany had to show the rest of the world how the National Social state could host with great efficiency such an international show piece. Significantly, however, Jewish people were not to be allowed to compete. Somehow Frank could not imagine the majority of people he had worked with being capable of these crimes against humanity.

At last the boat reaches New York almost on time and there is the welcome sight of his parents on the quayside. He is hugged by his mother whilst father greets him with a strong handshake. On the drive home he is questioned about his stay in Germany. His mother wants to know all about the food and accommodation—Did they feed him properly? Was he comfortable in his lodgings? Did he make friends? His father is very interested in the atmosphere in Germany—Did Frank feel that Hitler had the people behind him? Were the stories they had heard about the treatment of Jews true? What was their attitude towards the United States? Questions about his time at IG Farben could wait. Frank did not mention Helga, that too could wait.

7

"DAY OF INFAMY"

After a long sleep Frank goes down to have breakfast to be asked so many questions by his father about his experiences at IG Farben. He recounts how much he has learned of the industry and chillingly describes how the firm is so geared to the war industry with regular visits from high-ranking officers from all the services and leading politicians. He particularly recalls all the excitement there was when Hermann Goering came with a squad of uniformed officers. Goering himself wore a particularly garish, not to say vulgar, uniform of his own design to show his importance. Frank had found it hard to believe that this corpulent, rotund man had been a heroic "figure" in the First World War as an ace fighter pilot. He was glad to have been summoned home, apart that is of course from having to leave Helga. Some of IG Farben's industrial methods seemed much in advance of those he had been used to having being taught at university.

He has a week's rest before he goes to the factory where he meets several people whom he has known from his vacation jobs there. They are engrossed in listening to his experiences of a stay in a country preparing for war. Questions come flooding about the Nazis, about their gift for propaganda and ostentatious exhibitionism, but above all there is obvious fascination for the Führer himself. Initially, he had seemed a figure of fun as caricatured by Charlie Chaplin in "The Great Dictator," but nobody was laughing now! Were all Germans in such thrall as they had appeared to be in those films of the Nuremburg rallies?

Of course, away from the serious side, his younger colleagues wanted to know about German girls. Did they all have long blond hair in pigtails or plaited? Had he known many? Had he done "it"? Had he made many conquests? Normally he would have boasted about how many he had made, with suitable exaggerations, as is the wont with young men. He refused to answer that, but did admit that he had become quite keen on a certain Helga. "Quite keen," he thought to himself, rather an understatement! By now he had brought up the subject with his parents who naturally wanted to know just how close he felt. He was bolder in speaking as another person, so he tried to stop further questioning by answering in German: "Das ist nichts, wir sind nur gut befreundet." Good friends indeed!

In fact what has been so upsetting to him has been the lack of communication with her since returning home. He has written several times to her, but there has been no response. What does this mean? Has she lost interest? Are letters between Germany and the United States now forbidden? Although the USA is seen as possible ally of Great Britain, there is no formal state of war as they are neutral. He cannot bear to think she no longer has feelings for him after those declarations of undying love when he left Bremen. His parents have often teased him about his unusual enthusiasm in seeing what the postman has brought. "I do not see any German stamps there, my son," his father often says with a sly smile on his face as Frank hands over the usual official letters, gas bills, invoices, reminders etc., etc.

Frank then resumes his university studies for a further year before graduating in 1940. He passes comfortably but not with flying colours. His experience in Germany has been of great benefit to him, as a student and as a person. He has learned so much about his subject and about people. "Don't judge a book by its cover," is an expression which constantly recurs to him as it was a favourite of his liberal — minded English teacher at college. Although much of what had happened in Germany had been frightening, his meetings with individuals had been mostly friendly and a common word in letters home had been "freundlich" in describing people whom he had met.

He then enters into a minor managerial position at his father's factory but is placed in a different sector which suits both of them as he must learn about the business unaided. He is proving to be a very promising young man with definite potential. He does not neglect his sporting talents and plays basketball and baseball as well as football. His social life is as what one would expect from a young man with personality and sociability. There are dances to go to, professional sport to watch and naturally he is still attracted to girls as they are to him. Although he has dates with a few of them, one of whom he finds particularly "affectionate," he has not found one yet to equal Helga.

With President Roosevelt by force of personality having overcome the opponents of America's entry into the war, it becomes quite obvious that the USA will soon be involved. This happens sooner than expected when the Japanese treacherously attack Pearl Harbour whilst discussing peace in Washington on December 7th, 1941, "a day of infamy" as the President calls it. Adolf Hitler then makes the great mistake several days later by declaring war on the United States. At last Great Britain has another strong ally in addition to Soviet Russia in the fight against Fascism.

The entry of the United States into the war had caused contrasting attitudes towards its new enemies on the opposite oceans. On the Pacific coast there was great panic that the Japanese living there who were now American citizens would sabotage American installations and aid any Japanese invasion. Consequently, over 100.000 of them were moved from their family homes and moved into parts of the country far from the coast. They were re-housed in what were in effect prison camps, complete with barbed wire, in remote areas of such places as Arizona or Utah. The conditions were appalling with only the most basic of toilet facilities. Strangely enough those Japanese living in Hawaii, much closer to the action, were not subjected to the same treatment with fewer than 2,000 being treated as prisoners. It is odd that the same conditions were not imposed upon the Germans or Italians who had become US citizens.

On the Atlantic coast there was incredible complacency. The towns along the seaboard seemed blissfully unaware of the need for a blackout giving German U-Boats wonderful targets as the mainly merchant shipping was silhouetted against the lights.

There were no plans in place for escorting all these vital ships against such attacks, nor any system of convoys. Millions of tons of allied shipping were lost in the first few months after the American entry into the war before they belatedly re-acted to the danger.

8

AIRCREW TRAINING AND ROMANCE

As with thousands of other young men Frank answers the call to arms. He has already enlisted in the army air force reserve corps and with some reluctance as a one–time pacifist, volunteers for full-time service. His father with his German background has misgivings, but he is now a citizen of the United States and accepts his decision. Surely the love affair with Helga is now doomed.

With his educational background he is considered suitable for training as a pilot. He has mixed feelings as he is sent to an Air Force classification centre to see if he is suitable to be trained for such a demanding and responsible role.

There is a sense of excitement at this new challenge, but also he is very nervous as he keeps wondering if he will be good enough. He faces strenuous tests from doctors and psychologists: eye tests, co-ordination, mental ability, personality, re-action speeds. Frank finds the experience gruelling. The air force was desperately looking for candidates to train as pilots, navigators and bombardiers with half those initially chosen failing to meet the demanding standards.

Having passed the first stage, Frank is sent to a training school for potential pilots which he finds extremely hard work as so far he has had a fairly comfortable life, except for bursts of study with exams approaching at university. There is a six week course to begin with when the men are taught how to become soldiers. There is physical training with cross-country runs and work with weights, map work, drill on the square, orienteering, weapon training, marksmanship and military procedures. They have hardly any time to themselves but learn to have respect for their instructors except one whom Frank loathes. He is a sergeant called Payne—an apt name—who has a dreadful chip on his shoulder. He is from Tennessee in the south and doesn't like northern boys, especially those with university backgrounds. "You bloody Yankees with a posh education ain't nuttin to me and I'll show you what's what in this man's army." They have a great emphasis on formal parades, cadets saluting with swords, and close order drill being prominent features. He is finding it hard work, but he has to admit it is becoming enjoyable.

The next parts of the training programme are the Primary, Basic and Advanced levels at three different bases to be followed by a ten week post-graduate course — that is assuming each of the cadets passes each part to come out as a second lieutenant. Again the course requires exceptional concentration and mental and physical stamina. Frank does not get through the Basic part but is considered suitable material to be sent to train as a navigator. He is sent to the school for navigators in Hondo, Texas. This is a rather desolate spot surrounded by desert and there is little time for a social life, but he does manage to meet Maria, a dark-haired beauty from a Mexican family. This is an area where Spanish is a common language and he quickly becomes fairly competent in using it. After Helga, he now has another beautiful language tutor.

Ah, Helga! What has happened to her? She is never too far from his thoughts, but he cannot think that they will meet again as they cannot even communicate by letter. He often wonders if she has a new boyfriend. With her looks and personality she must have.

Maria works in a bar in the town, a bar whose trade has multiplied since the arrival of the air force.

Although he is usually a confident boy, at home with women, when he first sees her he feels rather nervous about chatting to her. She is probably twenty or so, has beautiful black, shiny hair, deep brown eyes, a very narrow waist and a shapely bosom. How perfect she would be for the opera "Carmen," he thinks. She must have a boyfriend and the jealousy of Latin races is well-known; he doesn't want a knife in his ribs. However, he does make as if to go over to buy a drink, encouraged by his raucous mates who call him "lover boy" and often ask him about Helga in phoney German accents and tease him about being a traitor to Uncle Sam. At last his courage returns, especially after his mates have questioned his reputation with women which they have heard about but not witnessed. His initial nervousness overcome, he starts a conversation with her but realises she is a little wary of all these airmen who repeatedly cast lascivious glances in her direction. Frank's aim now is to show what a "good guy" he is, not like the others! He talks to her about his life in the north, his university career, and his enlisting in the air force. Most of all, however, she is fascinated to hear about his German experience and life there under Hitler which to Texans seems almost on another planet. Did he have a girlfriend there and does he have one now? Without going into too many details he tells her about Helga, but says he has no particular one in America.

She then tells him that being a Mexican immigrant in Texas could be very difficult. They were a downtrodden minority restricted mainly to menial jobs, were discriminated against and in certain cases were segregated in restaurants, swimming pools, parks and often even in schools. There were signs at public swimming pools such as: "Tuesday reserved for negroes or Mexicans." All this was a result of a long-standing hostility when America had defeated Mexico in a war and then gone on to seize territory from them which was now part of the United States. Frank had not realised the extent of this problem. Although the arrival of the military had been good for trade, he realised why there was still a sense of hostility from some of the older people. "This can't be Germany all over again, can it?" he thought with a wry smile.

As the course was to last for eighteen weeks he did have the opportunity to see Maria quite often, even though the authorities were not too well disposed to airmen having friendships with local girls, nor were too many of their parents. He became very fond of her and loved hearing her speak in a half-Spanish, half-Texan language. Apart from her beauty, she was also excellent company with a great sense of ironic humour, mainly directed at the United States and its so-called democracy and equality for all. Her grandfather is always saying that President

Roosevelt's so-called New Deal does not seem to have reached them.

He goes for a walk with her one evening, puts his arm round her and kisses her passionately. Maria responds with equal feeling. They hug each other as though they will never come apart and carry on kissing intimately. It seems now that all thoughts of Helga are forgotten. She tells him that as soon as she first saw him that he was "Amor a primera vista." I have wondered when you were going to do that!" The evening could have gone on for ever, but Frank looks at his watch and realises that he should be back in camp by now. The discipline is strong and too many breaches could lead to dismissal from the course. Hurriedly, he suggests a further date which she says she will try to keep. Luckily for him when he returns to camp, the guard on duty is a sporting colleague on the football team and after a quick look around lets him in.

Although Frank is a graduate, he finds the course extremely testing and therefore the time allocated to sport is so relaxing after the lecture theatre and the initial test flights. His football skills have not deserted him and he becomes a key player on the base football team. In the lecture room he has to be proficient in all the different methods of navigation: pilotage, dead reckoning, radio, celestial, instrument calibration and a combination of any or all of these skills. The instrument calibration is particularly demanding as he has to be expert with the altimeter, all compasses, airspeed indicators, alignment of the astro-compass, astrograph, drift meter and check on the navigator's sextant and watch. There is a great amount of team work involved. With the pilot he has to study the flight plan of the route to be flown, examine closely the likely weather, tell him what type of navigation is intended to be used, work out what type of communication to be used in flight and synchronize the watches.

He must know how each part of the plane functions: as well as the pilot he has close cooperation with the wireless operator, must be able to use and service a 0.50 calibre machine gun at his post, must know how to operate all the turrets, radio equipment and oxygen supplies, and in fact be able to take over any post in the plane in an emergency. A navigation cadet logged about one hundred hours in the air, but for every hour of flight he spent five in the classroom. Actual test flying he is finding relatively less confusing, although the first flight when he had to navigate from Hondo to Lubbock air field in Texas he found very nerve-racking. The pilot, Lt. Anders from Virginia, however encouraged him by saying that he had done a good job for a first-timer. He soon finds out when he returns to base that many B-I7s crash in training flights.

He finds it quite easy to make friends as there is a bond between all these young men, all of whom, as with him, are volunteers. They have a deep sense of patriotism and also like the thought of wearing a smart officer's uniform, a sure magnet for girls. Many of them had volunteered to escape the infantry, but also there was great glamour in flying in a country that was becoming very conscious of the growth of the influence of aerial power. The recent civil war in Spain had shown the world just how important was the strength of air forces as German and Italian planes had been used to great effect to aid the fascist Franco. They could even demolish a town as with Guernica, a lesson which the leaders in the Pentagon duly noted.

Frank's friends came from all over the United States and speaking to them was an education in itself. There was Paul Heineke, 20, 2nd. Year Law student from Pennsylvania who had "for the duration" given up his studies; Charlie Andrews, 23, school-teacher from Tennessee; Andy Jacobs, 19, straight from high school in Michigan, who becomes "Junior" and Loren Frye, 25, salesman from California. Loren was naturally known as "Daddy" and lost no time in telling the others that they were just kids who knew nothing about the big, outside world. He would tell them stories about his travels on the road, the wonderful deals he had done, the range of characters he had met, his amazing home near Los Angeles and his experiences with beautiful, willing dames. Whilst Andy listened with wide-eyed amazement, Charlie butted in, "Don't listen to him, kid. He ain't no Clark Gable; he's just a bull-shitter."

All this was said in good humour and either in the barrack room or in Maria's bar there was many a lively discussion. Apart from Andy, they could all be opinionated, in politics, football, types of women preferred or the course they were on. There was naturally some raking over of the Civil War between Frank and Paul on one side and Charlie on the other with Loren acting as referee. However, whatever were the rights and wrongs, all agreed that it was a disaster when members of the same family could turn against each other. They had all seen the recently released "Gone With The Wind" and Charlie had even read Margaret Mitchell's novel.

As one would expect, the subject of women dominates most of the conversations, with all of them having their fantasies of Hollywood stars.

"Gee, what would I give for a night with Lana Turner!" sighs Paul.

Loren retorts," Come off it. You wouldn't know what to do with her. Anyway, I met a blonde in San Francisco just as good as her and she wanted to marry me."

"I think that we can ignore that one. You say you were a great salesman, but none of us is taken in by that stuff."

"Give me Rita Hayworth, I just love redheads," is Charlie's contribution to the on-going debate.

"Just a minute, we haven't heard what Junior has to say yet, have we?"

"Don't be so cruel, Loren. The lad's a bit shy. Hey Frank, has that Maria of yours any friends who can sort of, you know, induct, Junior into the pleasures of life."

"Leave me out of it, I don't need to fantasise about Hollywood like you guys—I had Helga in Germany and now I've got my dark-haired beauty here. Leave the kid alone. He probably knows more about it than all you put together. Don't blush, Junior, you're a good-looker, which is more than can be said for any of these misfits here, except me, of course!"

They have an excellent supply of magazines with pictures of all the great movie stars: Betty Grable, Susan Hayward, Joan Crawford, Clark Gable, Spencer Tracy, James Stewart etc. The sight of them and all the Hollywood glamour makes them homesick as they think of all the times they have seen their movies when at home.

There are also the great bands of the day to listen to on the radio: Artie Shaw; Benny Goodman; Harry James and Glenn Miller. Again, each one of these bands has vociferous support.

And so these discussions go on, some of more of a serious nature, at times quite academic as befitted their background, but many like this one which ease their tension. If they pass out and are given a commission as a 2nd lieutenant with the coveted wings, who knows where they would be sent? It could be the Pacific where their buddies were steadily pushing back the Japs, or to the European theatre of war from where they had heard stories of how London and other big cities and ports were being heavily bombed. The newspapers had been full of stories of the Battle of Britain, the name of Winston Churchill was continually the subject of articles with his American mother somehow gaining credit.

9

PASSES OUT AS 2ND LIEUTENANT

Frank continues to see Maria whenever he can get a pass. One night when she had finished work early, he meets her secretly away from where people gathered. That is secret except for a Sergeant/ Mechanic with whom he had struck up a friendship on the football field. He showed him how to gain access to his office in the hangar when the only other being there would be a giant silver B-17 Fortress in for engine overhaul. Maria is rather nervous about being on military property, especially in these circumstances. Frank says that Sgt. Conroy will look out for them. After some idle conversation, he can no longer restrain himself and gently eases her on to the mattress which Cliff Conroy keeps for off-duty spells. She teases him asking what his intentions are. His answer is to kiss her full on the lips. There is a very passionate reaction as she clutches him ever more tightly. Freeing her left hand, she feels him on his groin which causes him to shiver with pleasure. She is wearing a most seductive perfume which arouses him even further. He pulls her thin blouse over her shoulders before taking off her bra and kissing her erect nipples. My God, what a perfect bosom she has, better than Grable's, he thinks. Maria has her head back as she groans with passion and begs him not to stop now. He has a condom which she slides on for him. She is not wearing any knickers and he quickly enters her. As they rock rhythmically in unison, he has to stop her from screaming out as she achieves orgasm. This has been even better for him than sex with Helga all that time ago. Unlike Helga she is not a virgin and knows how to please a man. A few minutes later his thoughts turn perversely to his German girl-friend. What is she doing now? Could it be the same thing with a handsome, young fair-haired German soldier or member of the Luftwaffe. He feels unreasonable jealousy at the thought. Maria is wondering if they will meet again, or now that he has had what he wanted, will he disappear?

He looks at his watch and after a final passionate kiss and adjusting his uniform, decides he had better call in at the bar before returning to camp. Maria returns by a different route to her home. She has of course been with friends! His friends naturally ask him where he has been, having noted that Maria has also been absent from the bar. When he says that he has been cleaning his kit for the next day's inspection, Loren asks him with a slight smile on his lips, "Exactly what kit are we talking about?" Frank ignores this innuendo and stresses the importance of being well-turned out as potential officers.

"Knock it off Frank, don't come on with that with us! We don't blame you, who wouldn't want a bit of, shall we say, entertainment, with that dame?" Loren persists. Even Junior smiles at this.

They make it back to the camp just before the gates are closed. This time there is no friendly guard on duty but a rather fierce sergeant. John Brady from the Bronx is in charge of security and there is no taking liberties with him. Stories of him are legion; he has been a regular army man for over twenty years, much of them spent in the Philippines. He looks upon young potential officers as beneath him and makes the most of his power over them until the time comes when they have to be saluted. His drills on the parade ground are very exacting. He once asked the squad to do an about turn. Unfortunately one of the group carried straight on. "Butler, what the 'effin Hell do you think you are doing? I didn't know you'd been given a leave pass. Report to guard room and get your pass—to do five days of fatigues

!" All of this delivered in a raucous, very aggressive tone. Of course Butler swears to himself to get his own back when he becomes an officer, as all soldiers in such a position threaten, but never actually do.

This type of NCO comes from a certain section of humanity which doesn't seem to belong anywhere else. It is hard to imagine them in everyday civilian jobs when there could be nobody to shout at to the full extent of their vocal chords. It is true that they are always very smartly turned out with a crease on their trousers looking so sharp you feel you could almost cut your fingers on it and a shine on their boots which could act as a mirror—that would appeal to Frank!—as they stand ramrod straight. They all seem to be "hard" men, a vital quality in a soldier. When all is said and done, they are the ones you would want with you in the trenches. Being brought up in such a tough area of New York has obviously had a significant effect on Brady's character.

They return to their billets and retire almost immediately to bed as the CO, Lt. Colonel George Ford from Oklahoma, is going to inspect them the following morning.

George Ford was a regular with twenty years' service. He was a West Point graduate who had passed out high in his year group. Son of a senator for Oklahoma, he is a tall, handsome man with thick greying hair, a Ronald Colman moustache and an air of authority. Although he is necessarily strict, he is much respected by the men as he is always fair and honest, a man they feel they could approach if there were any problems. He had served at different posts, including Pearl Harbor, but he was thought ideal by Washington to take over an officer training station. He had come to Major-General Eaker's attention by his enthusiasm for Billy Mitchell's philosophy on the great importance of the bomber in planning warfare. He was a student of the topic and had written a well-received thesis on the subject at Staff College which had marked him down as a man for future promotions. Helping to turn these young men into highly-trained officers would look good on his service record.

After the sergeant-major brings the parade to attention, the CO gives a talk about what it meant to be an officer in the USAAF. They had heard such addresses before from officers of different ranks, but as the time for graduating is approaching they concentrate more than ever. They are told that they are the cream of the country's talents, along with the pilots and bombardiers. "Never let your country down in the air or on the ground. You young men are what the country needs in this time of peril for the future of democracy." After a few more words on similar lines, the colonel takes the salute as they pass by in formation to the strains of their signature tune "Off We Go Into the Wild Blue Yonder." Even the cynics amongst them admitted that listening to this raised the hairs on the back of their necks and brought out goose pimples.

The course is nearing its end now and if and when they pass, they will be given postings to who knows where? It could be staying in the States, going to the Pacific theatre, Iceland perhaps or Europe i.e. the United Kingdom. The intensity does not let up in the repetition of the course work in the classroom, the physical training and, of course, the flying by night and day.

To Frank's disappointment, he never sees Maria again. He tells himself it is because she cannot bear the thought of his leaving, perhaps never to see him again. On the other hand, she could be waiting for the next group of officer candidates to come to the camp and see what handsome ones she can meet. Frank has no doubt that there will be plenty of admirers. His ego drives these thoughts from his mind — no, she will not be able to cope with the disappointment. Still, it was great when he knew her and she was a wonderful lover. Let's put it down to experience. In any case, he tells himself he prefers Helga; but will he ever see her again? He didn't even get an "Adios" or "Hasta la Vista!" from Maria he thinks as his mind flicks from one to the other of his girl-friends.

The time passes quickly until their final parade when all those who were to receive their commissions, that is the great majority of those who started the course, are assembled on the tarmac. The ceremony starts with the band playing the "Stars and Stripes" which is followed by some two-star general from the Pentagon inspecting them and offering his congratulations after he has given them a suitable address from the platform. He more or less reiterates much of what they have already heard, but coming from such a high-ranking person it seems to be even more memorable.

They march away to the USAAF band playing their signature tune which is very appropriate in these circumstances as their destination is as yet unknown. It causes further emotions to hear these patriotic tunes. How proud they all are to be wearing the distinctive gold wings of a newly-fledged navigator and the silver bar of a 2nd Lieutenant on their epaulette.

10

POSTED TO UK

When they return to their huts, they are eager to read what their postings have been. For some reason this information has been delayed until now. All are eager to tell each other what they have been given. There are different reactions. Some are not pleased to be given a home posting to train new navigators, when they wanted to see some action; others are rather apprehensive when finding out that they will have to go to the Pacific Theatre to fight the Japs, but some of these selected for this onerous task have more of a Gung-Ho attitude of, "Let's give those Nip, yellow bastards a taste of their own medicine. Remember Pearl!" Frank is one of those to be posted to the UK, which is looked upon as possibly the best one to be given. He is very pleased that Charlie Andrews, his schoolteacher friend, all North/ South rivalry forgotten, has also received this posting.

He has read so much about England in particular, not just about the war. In his university course he has read about the great unemployment problems of the 30s, not that his own country was free from such troubles. He also summons to his mind the old traditions he was told about in his history lessons at college: Royalty; the Tudor kings and queens, especially Henry VIII with his wives; the great buildings in London and the aristocracy, something unknown in his own country. Of course, it will be good to bring up how George Washington drove Britain out of the states, but on second thoughts that may not be too tactful! He has heard that the Limeys can be a bit sensitive in this area and that they are also much more formal than American citizens. Hell, he knows all about that from his stay in Germany.

He has now dismissed Maria from his thoughts as he is still upset by her refusal to meet him after that night of passion, and in any case Helga starts to come back to his mind. What is she doing now? He has heard of heavy raids on Bremen by the RAF. What a situation he is in now, still thinking so much about, and yes, being in love with, an enemy citizen. Helga, an enemy, it doesn't bear thinking about. All those lovely walks round Bremen and learning so much about it. The trip she took him on to Hamburg is also one of his greatest memories. The greatest, however, is the night they made love in Frau Lütze's house. Helga became a complete woman on that night. He wonders if the good Frau ever found out. It bothers him that she could have a serious boyfriend, or even be married! What business of his is it in any case?

There is a sense of leaving college as they say their farewells to all the permanent staff on the camp. There are all the technicians, experts who maintained the B-17s, mess waiters, lecturers, labourers and drivers. Then who can forget all those NCOs who cajoled, bullied and at times made their lives difficult, but all in a good cause to make proper officers and gentlemen out of them. Last of all they visit Lt. Col. George Ford, their much-respected commanding officer, who wishes them Good Luck with the hope that he and his men have helped to make them good airmen of whom their country can be proud.

They have now been allocated to crews for the flight over to the UK. With Frank there will be Jim Broad, pilot aged 22, from Sacramento, California; Larry Gomes, 20, bombardier, native of Grand Rapids, Minnesota; Harry Schultz, co-pilot 21, from Lexington, Virginia and Gerry Jackson, aged 21, an extra pilot for re-assignment in England. He is a native of Orlando, Florida. These are all, or going to be, professional men on their return home, in law, business or education.

They go to their favourite bar for a last evening's entertainment before setting off early the next morning. They will then be en route for their allocated postings, whether they are in the States or abroad. As can be expected, it is rather a rowdy evening with the drinks flowing. Although Maria is missing, there is no shortage of attractive feminine company as it is well-known locally that this is the last night of this group of officer cadets. Whilst not exactly a Roman orgy, the mixture of alcohol and a highly sex-charged atmosphere does make for some interesting sights. Many a couple try to sneak off outside surreptitiously to have a last farewell with those they have met previously or just on the night; Frank is still sulking about Maria's seeming rejection of him. After such a night of passion when she was so willing, how can she have so forsaken him? Pedro, the bar owner, states that he has never seen so many "Borrachos, en mi bar." It is true that it would be hard to found a sober man or woman.

Although they have been given some extra leeway as it is their last night, it has now come to the time to leave and return to the camp. Amongst the men there have been many friendships formed with promises of keeping in touch. How many of these will be honoured, especially when one thinks of the future in the skies over the Pacific and Europe. They have had a hard night's drinking, been engaged in other activities and some will require an early morning start, but most of them find it so difficult to fall asleep. Many become very sentimental about their parting — the sense of bonding required by the air force has certainly worked here.

There has just been one "outsider" in the group, Mitchell Johnson from Idaho, who had complained about nearly everything from start to finish: the food, the night exercises, the lateness of mail, the discipline, even the rowdiness of his colleagues. He had been told in no uncertain terms that he was not exactly popular.

"If you have this attitude, why the f . . . don't you pack up your bags and leave? We're so fed-up with your continual f . . . . moaning that you're lucky we haven't reported you to those above for being detrimental to morale. Go and kick ass somewhere else."

"How the hell do you think you're going to become a navigator with this attitude?"

"Imagine your pessimism and negative attitude in a run over Germany or some Pacific island. What effect is this going to have on the rest of your buddies?"

However, as the weeks went by his attitude improved and the reason for his attitude became clear. From being a young boy, inspired by reading about the Wright Brothers and Billy Mitchell, he had desperately wanted to be a pilot. Failing the course and being transferred to the navigational branch had hurt him and seemed like some sort of relegation, especially as he had a father who was driven with ambition for his son. How marvellous for him to boast to his golf club friends that young Mitchell was a pilot in the USAAF! Mitchell was embarrassed by his behaviour and made a fulsome apology to his colleagues. They were very pleased to hear him say this. There are many types of courage, the most obvious being in battle which is what these young men could be about to face; however, Mitchell showed a different kind of courage in owning up to his mistake and changing his attitude so that he became a welcome member of the group and not so much a loner. He buckled down to try to become an efficient navigator which he did.

On this last night many of them go over past topics which had been heard ad nauseam, but it does them good to air these sentiments again. So many have feelings of homesickness and make their state, whether it be the coast, the rolling plains, the mountains, the Fall, or the wild life seem like Paradise or God's little acre. Their families again come into play with their wonderful mothers, fathers and siblings. They detail their romances with some being brave enough to admit their virginity and others coming out with unlikely, oft-repeated stories of their exploits with beautiful girls. Frank, of course, has had such experiences but says little about Helga, now an enemy, out of respect. He is the only one who has had experience of living abroad for any length of time and has had many stories to tell of life in the Third Reich, with a little embellishment at times.

All those who have been posted to the 100th Bomb Group in the UK fly to Kearney Airfield in Nebraska. After more check-ups and talks from high-ranking officers they depart the following morning. Frank and all those bound for the UK fly to Iceland first of all in a B-17 navigated by his best pal, Charlie, and land at Reykjavik after a few hours' flight. They had been warned about it, but were still amazed at the Icelandic landscape as they approached: miles of volcanic rock, very little vegetation, few signs of life and although it was summer, what seemed like permanent snow on the mountains. They felt sorry for their colleagues in the forces who had been posted there.

Landing at Keplavik was just like landing in an outpost of The United States. It had been built mainly by the US military for operating heavy bombers and there was also a fighter strip. It had been opened in early 1943 and was thus just about in use when Frank and his colleagues land there on their way to the UK.

They have time for a reasonable meal there before continuing their flight, with Frank this time as navigator.

As they approach the UK groans can be heard from passengers, especially Frank as navigator. All those stories they have heard about Britain's climate are coming true: there is very heavy cloud with poor visibility — what a baptism on active service! They are diverted from the intended Scottish airport to a place called Burtonwood, near Manchester.

This is a huge depot for all the American air forces in Britain and Frank is glad to have successfully landed his passengers there unscathed. All around them as they land are hundreds of packing cases, lorries of all sizes, tankers, armoured vehicles ready to be assembled, parts of planes and what seems like hundreds of Jeeps scurrying round like ants from a recently disturbed nest. You can see countless GIs of all ranks from private to fairly senior officers and all seem so busy. Here is the United States' arsenal for whenever the anticipated invasion of Europe takes place. All the men in Frank's plane are overwhelmed by the size and scope of all they see — their country is obviously at war and means business.

They are due to stay here for two or three days whilst their B-17 is overhauled before continuing their trip to some other unheard of place further south. The nearest town is something like Warrington, another strange sounding place. They are told, however, that the big cities of Manchester and Liverpool are fairly close. These they have heard of in geography lessons at college, with Liverpool doing so much cross Atlantic trade with the USA in the cotton industry and Manchester being the cotton centre of great importance.

When they have had sufficient rest, Frank and Charlie decide to get hold of a jeep and drive into this place called Warrington, which they emphasised on the long drawn-out first syllable. They find a parking lot and go into the first place they find which sells beer. There are already a few of their countrymen there who are very inquisitive. They are mostly enlisted men who are a little taken aback as they see the officers' bars on their uniform for this is a place for other ranks. However, neither Frank nor Charlie feel themselves above talking to these men as they rely so much upon them when in the air as part of their crew or on the ground as the highly-skilled technicians who service their planes; without such men their lives would be in great danger before they even took off.

These men are from all over the States and the different dialects are fascinating to listen to, the most colourful that of those from the Deep South. "Can you translate that into real English?" Frank said more than once when listening to a fitter from Georgia or an electrician from Alabama. They are mostly ground crew who are permanently stationed at Burtonwood, but there are many aircrew, such as gunners or wireless operators who are also waiting to go on a posting somewhere in the UK.

They are told all about Warrington and the life there from the "regular citizens", which seemed something of a contradiction in terms as the electrician from Alabama, Lyndon Taft, outlined it. There were bars, or pubs as the local natives called them, dance halls, fish and chip shops, something new to them, but the town itself was nothing to get excited about. If you wanted a proper hamburger, you had to stay on the base. One good thing they were informed was that the girls there were very friendly, especially if you gave them a pair of real silk stockings. "That's good to hear," says Charlie," pity we ain't goin' to be here too long." You had to get used to the local accent, however, which was nothing like the English they had heard before.

It is soon time to move on as they climb into their Flying Fortresses for the next stage of the journey to glory, or whatever! It is now summer 1943.

11

INTO BATTLE FROM NORFOLK

After being used to flying over the vast plains, mountains and forests of the United States, the men cannot get over how soon they arrive at their airfield in East Anglia. They have been told in Warrington that their base was at the other end of the country and here they are less than two hours later. They have been struck by the number of what looked like floating silver whales in the skies near the big cities. These they were informed were known as barrage balloons, designed to catch enemy planes in their tentacles and bring them down, or at least keep them at a height where their bombing would be less accurate.

As they approach their destination it strikes them all just how flat the land is and how many airfields they pass over. Jim Broad, the 22-yr.-old pilot, remarks on this sight," Just like a gigantic aircraft-carrier, boys. Sure hope can bring this beauty down safe and sound and not be shown up by those navy guys or my kid brother in destroyers will let me know all about it!"

They discover that their base is called Thorpe Abbotts in the county of Norfolk where they touch down on June 9th. As you would expect, there are not many signs of habitation on first landing for as in the USA, they are used to great areas of space far from towns for their airfield. In the wide open spaces of their homeland the airfields are usually far from civilisation with entry strictly limited to forces personnel or those on official business. They will soon become accustomed to the locals being almost part of the scene on the camp sites. There are no guards on the roads approaching the site and amazingly the local people are free to wander round and stare at these exciting aircraft parked so close to the road. There is never any trouble for civilians to walk across the fields and approach the dispersal points. They soon notice on closer inspection that there is a very small village right next to the planes. On those hardstandings for parking the bombers opposite the control tower it seems as though the rear gunner of the Forts is next to the back rooms of the houses.

They are shown to their accommodation which they find is rather basic. There are damp Nissen huts surrounded by mud with eight beds along each side. There is a stove in the middle which they don't need now as it is summer, but the old-timers tell them it isn't much good in winter anyway, except for those tough guys who came from the mountainous states like Colorado or Wyoming. The toilets are primitive and the showers some distance away.

"Hell, if we are given these facilities, what do the enlisted guys get?" complains Larry Gomes.

"You fellows are nearly in Canada, so you should be familiar with deprivation," quips Harry Schultz.

"I didn't expect luxury when I volunteered for Uncle Sam's flyboys, but this is the pits," states Gerry Jackson.

Frank thought that he had seen better housing in the poorer parts of New York.

Harry Schultz sympathises with Frank: "You, a posh boy from Pennsylvania, must feel it more than we hicks from the sticks," and so the criticism goes on, but inwardly they feel proud that they had been made officers in such an elite body as the USAAF.

The 500th, however, has gained something of a reputation for ill-discipline in training and has undergone some changes in leadership as a result. This news has preceded them and leads to unwelcome, not to say very sarcastic, remarks from those airmen already on site. They have gained themselves the title of The Bloody Hundredth as a result of their casualties in action. The original crews it must be admitted had a very casual approach to flying discipline and keeping in formation.

The time has come for serious action and nine of the crews, including Frank's, are detailed to go on a practise run the following day to become accustomed to formation flying and to carrying a full bomb load. After receiving a briefing from Major Phillips, they are to fly to Dishforth, an RAF airfield in Yorkshire, after veering out over The North Sea. The leading navigator, not Frank to his disappointment mixed with a little jealousy, is told the bearings, distance and weather for the trial flight.

The flight passes without too much difficulty except for one or two bursts of anti-aircraft gunfire from batteries somewhere near Hull. It is evident, however, that they soon realise their error as B-17s are not like any known enemy plane and were not flying at any great height. On their return to base they are full of far-fetched stories of being in serious action. The main news to impart on their de-briefing is that their trial flight over England had been successful.

They are then informed that the plane they have flown in will be theirs for action and that the crew will be the same. Frank's fellow flyers will be those with whom he flew across the Atlantic. In addition to the pilots and bombardier he will have a cross-section of American society as enlisted men. rear-gunner Billy Cipriani, 21, Italian from New Jersey, a would-be musician; waist-gunners, Sgts. Geoff. Speer and Mark Kasprowicz, 20 and 19, one of German extract, the other Polish, both railroad employees, Geoff from Rhode Island and Mark from Indiana ; upper gun turret, S/Sgt Hank Crosby, 20, apprentice dental technician from Florida and ball turret, Sgt. Wayne Bridges, 22, from Idaho, unemployed salesman.

It is time now for serious business and to prepare for their first flight over enemy territory. The crew are awakened at 0300 hours by the duty orderly and told to be at the operations room straightaway to be prepared for a mission. The stomach cramps and nerves are working really hard at this thought of being in action over Europe. Would all this hard training back in the States, all those courses attended, all those arduous cross-country runs have fitted them for this, the ultimate aim? Would the crew have the necessary team spirit of all for one to bind them as an effective unit? Only time will tell, thinks Frank as they make their way over for their briefing. They would have to justify their silver bars or stripes.

It is a fairly warm June morning and the atmosphere is dramatic as they enter the Group Ops room. Just inside the door is a chaplain who makes

Frank think of "Nearer My God To Thee" and other religious lines he had heard at college. American Red Cross girls supply them with coffee and light refreshments. Even though they are soon to have breakfast, they are still very grateful as of course they have a few seconds to speak to these pretty girls. Inside his friends go as near the front as they are permitted for the front rows are reserved for the higher-ranking officers. They are becoming nervous as they start to sweat which isn't helped by wearing their fleece-lined flying jackets. On the stage are easels; on the back is a huge map of Europe. Where will they be going? From the rear of the hall comes the Group Adjutant, a very thin man with red, receding hair. He is rather older than the crews and calls them to attention to announce the arrival of the higher ranking officers.

First there is the CO, a full colonel, graduate of Harvard and West Point who saw action in The First World War on the Western Front over Belgium. He is followed in strict order by the Air Executive, the Group Ops officer and the squadron commanders. A Major Johnston, head of intelligence, pulls back the curtain with a flourish which he enjoys. There is a ribbon stretching from Norfolk to a port in western France. Thank God for that, at least it's not in Germany. The target is St. Nazaire, a base for the infamous U-Boats. They have been causing havoc with allied shipping crossing the

Atlantic, but they are starting to be mastered. The Group Operations Officer takes over. Major Rhodes stresses the seriousness of the operation. There will be no shortage of a warm welcome with their flak or close-by fighter bases. He gives details of the formation of the planes. Frank's will be in the high squadron.

Other officers then give details of bomb loads, ammunition for the gunners and forecast the expected weather. As they will be flying high, they are warned that their electrical underwear is essential. The Group Bombardier and Group Navigator tell the other bombardiers and navigators that they will have a special briefing. Frank and Larry go off to listen to their superiors. Frank is quite impressed by his "chief" who is so clear and business-like in laying out the details of the codes for the timings and places, the altitudes and the meeting points with the rest of the groups. They will be very high when they attack the target, so will they please check all their electrical flying gear before starting. "We don't want any of you jokers losing a hand or foot and getting a nice little one-way ticket back to stateside now, do we?" A few mumble that they wouldn't mind. They are due for take-off at 0.500 hours.

The next stop is the mess for some breakfast. There is an excellent meal awaiting them; bacon, eggs, pancakes, just like being back in the States.

Most tuck into their food with the thought that they not have many more such breakfasts, others are too nervous to be able to eat properly. Although Frank refuses to think that he could be a casualty, he is somewhat of a fatalist and has the attitude of what will be, will be.

They pile into the trucks to go to their planes, the B-17s, the pride of the USAAF. They are not called Flying Fortresses without reason as they are armed with machine guns, front, rear, upper turret, lower turret and each side of the fuselage. The flight formations are so arranged that they have a field of fire in all directions for protection against enemy fighters. The hierarchy had such faith in them that they were held to be perfectly capable of looking after themselves and so did not need too much fighter protection. Because of this belief, it was thought that they could carry out daylight bombing which would enable them to bomb vital targets with greater precision than the RAF who had given up this tactic after heavy losses and very moderate results. The Americans also thought that they could avoid civilian casualties by concentrating on important targets away from built-up areas as much as possible. To help them in their theories they had developed the miraculous Norden bombsight which it was claimed was so accurate that the bombardier could "drop a bomb in a pickle barrel."

Frank swings up through the hatch below the cockpit to show his athleticism, whilst most of the others take the easy way up the steps at the side of the fuselage. After extensive checks have been taken by the ground crew, they take off at 0500 hours as planned to rendezvous over The Wash at Splasher Six, their navigational meeting point for the bombers with other squadrons, before turning south-west towards the target. The lead navigator has the responsibility of guiding the air armada to their target; Frank being in the top flight is in the safest spot, the lead navigator's in the most dangerous.

German fighters usually make for this plane as it also has the lead bombardier and command pilot. They have recently adopted the tactic of flying head-on at the bombers, veering away at the last possible moment. It requires extraordinary skill and courage on the part of the Luftwaffe pilots and is a terrifying sight for those in the bomber's cockpit. Head-on collisions have not been unknown, sending eleven men to their death, ten in the bomber and the German pilot. Over the south of England two of the planes abort because of engine malfunction; as crews have to achieve twenty-five missions to be able to qualify for going to a desk job or to train new aircrew back in the States, this won't count for those ten men as a mission. Frank doesn't know whether he is sorry for them or envious; only time will tell.

They have now climbed 17,000 feet and it is exceptionally cold even with all that electrical clothing on. The oxygen masks are firmly in place. After leaving Cornwall behind, they have their first confrontation with the enemy. Two Focke-Wulf 190s appear from nowhere, fire a few desultory rounds and disappear back towards France. Well, if the enemy didn't know about their flight path already, they certainly will now. As they are approaching their target Frank knows the others will be feeling just like him, however much some may try to conceal it with bravado, that mixture of excitement, exhilaration even, together with a knotting of the stomach and bowel areas. This happens however many missions you have flown, Frank's crew are on their first. He has a fleeting thought of Helga. What would she be thinking now if she knew he was going to bomb, nay kill, some of her countrymen, he who had seemed to have made friends quite easily with them in 1939? How crazy was war! It is now time to dismiss these thoughts and concentrate on the task ahead.

The lead planes soon have St. Nazaire in sight and see black balls of smoke. The flak batteries have located them and are giving all they have. That Major Rhodes was certainly right, but "welcome" was certainly a word charged with irony. Frank's plane does the run-in and releases its bombs over the pens. The plane rises after losing all that weight.

All around they see that some of the planes have received hits with holes in the fuselage, tears in the wings or some of the engines are not functioning; Frank has not noticed any actually shot down though which is a great relief. It's time now to return home.

It's an even greater relief when the Spitfires can come within range and drive away the ME109s which have been pursuing them. They land back at base about two hours later, several of their colleagues coming in with serious damage and they hear of others who haven't yet made it. The B-17 is an extraordinarily sturdy aircraft and it is amazing how many survive to fly again.

The crews go to be de-briefed by the Intelligence Officer. They are optimistic in what they have achieved as there were so many direct hits on the pens. They are told that they have lost five planes, one flew as far as Cornwall and six parachutes were seen descending; as yet there is no news of the other four aircraft.

The men are shattered and most go straight to their beds, some not even bothering to take off their flying gear. Some ask the orderly to bring them doughnuts and strong coffee After he has recovered and taken some refreshment, Frank decides it is time he answered his parents' most recent letter which he received ten days ago.

His mother tells him the local gossip such as the girl two houses away marrying a marine she has only met very recently. He may be drafted to the Pacific theatre quite soon so this is a rushed marriage, something not uncommon in wartime. The area is making a great effort in selling war bonds with Dad being to the forefront in organisation. His mother is worried that he is doing too much as he is having more and more work thrust on him at the plant. They have just bought a dog, a golden Labrador which they have called Jasper—they can't believe the hairs he leaves behind him or the mess he makes, such as tearing up dad's slippers! However, he is a beautiful animal. Then comes the main part when she asks about what he is doing. His dad tells him how proud they are of him as are their neighbours and friends.

He doesn't want to say too much in case they worry. Next time he writes he promises he will tell them more about the people and countryside where he is. His colleagues have the makings of a good crew with a great sense of humour and their superiors are mainly good except for a Lt. Col. Thompson, a new arrival, who is a bit of a martinet, overdoing the discipline line. Frank doesn't want to mention the raid they have just been on to St Nazaire so as not to worry them. He thanks his dad for doing a great job, telling him how much the boys appreciate it as it makes them feel that the country is behind them.

12

REGENSBURG / SCHWEINFURT MISSIONS

Frank comes to realise that Col. Thompson could be right as in successive missions the casualties have been mounting ; the euphoria after the raid on the U-Boat pens has started to diminish. There has been a lack of discipline in keeping in formation which has been leading to the enemy fighters picking off the bombers more easily. When a plane becomes detached from the rest, the enemy fighters which have been hovering attack as hyenas do in the wild: they make for the weakest in the herd, a stray springbok or antelope and bring it down. The whole point of keeping together is to give the Forts a wide range of fire-power. There have been instances of gunners panicking and shooting down their own planes. Frank has also seen mid-air collisions when twenty men can be lost in one go.

On their days off the Colonel sometimes has them practising flying in tight formation and keeping on course. There have also been signs of untidiness in their rooms and in their lockers which can be an indicator of lowering morale. Thompson is determined to make them flyers to be proud of. There are sacrifices as those who are not considered of the required standard are sent on a refresher course. Frank's crew have so far survived in the actions and in the cull. They have five missions under their belt towards the magic twenty-five.

They are sitting in the camp cinema one August evening when the dreaded red light goes on. "All crews to Ops. Room immediately." Where can this one be to? On the way to the briefing the majority opinion is French railway yards or some fuel depots. They sit down chatting until the Group Adjutant calls them to attention. The senior officers file in with the tension growing. There is a gasp as after the CO's initial remarks, the curtain is pulled back to reveal a double mission: Schweinfurt and Regensburg which are deep into Germany. How much time are the German fighters, or bogeys, as they are known, going to have to prepare? The fighter escorts for the bombers can only go as far as the Belgian frontier with Germany which of course the enemy is well aware of.

Frank is on the Regensburg raid aiming for a very important Messerschmitt factory, the other groups are heading for Schweinfurt which is a key area for producing the absolutely essential ball bearings. The men are under no illusions about the magnitude of their task and the dangers involved. These raids into such a heavily defended area at such a great distance lead Frank and his colleagues to throw doubt on the wisdom of all these daylight attacks. There have been growing losses with these tactics. The plan is for twenty-one Forts from Thorpe Abbotts to take part in the mission with the rest of the group coming from other bases in East Anglia. The point of the Regensburg raid, apart from the obvious targets, is to draw away fighter aircraft from the more important mission to Schweinfurt.

Unfortunately the original plan for both groups to go almost simultaneously, so as to confuse the German defences does not work out as the bad weather delays the departure of the Schweinfurt force for several hours. This gives the enemy fighters confronting the Regensburg force plenty of time to refuel and re-arm to take on the latecomers.

All the way to the target they are attacked by German fighters and many are shot down before reaching there. Fortunately for some of the men they manage to bale out and, if lucky, become prisoners-of-war. However, many go down with their craft which are exploding, looking like great balls of orange, red and blue fire. He sees on the ground from a height of over 20,000 feet what he believes are red and blue flares before realising that they are in fact B-17s which have just been shot down and are blazing. The Regensburg force reaches its target which is relatively easy to find as it is all on one complex on an easily spotted bend on the Danube. It drops its bombs with a satisfactory degree of accuracy, fortunately hardly touching the hospital nearby which they knew about. They then set off flying, not to their base in England, but to North Africa by way of Italy. On their way they pass east of Munich before flying over some beautiful scenery in the Alps, including Lakes Chiemsee and Garda. The Dolomites are next on their way all of which makes the pilot speak for all of them when with a sigh he says, "Gee, I would sure like to visit this area in better times without feeling there could be a bandit on my tail." Several have to land in Italy, however, or in the sea as they run out of fuel, or have been very badly damaged. Some of these are rescued by a German boat, but most of the downed airmen are pulled out of the sea by friendly forces. They are met by sporadic gunfire over Italy and see some Italian fighters which do not engage them.

Upon arrival in Tunisia, 2Lt Eberhardt soon realises that many of their planes have been lost and many of those who come in have suffered serious damage and would need major repairs if they were to fly again. There was a high proportion that was without guns, ammunition or oxygen equipment as these had been thrown out over the Mediterranean to lighten the load and save fuel. Many men are suffering from various degrees of injury, especially burns and cuts. One of his crew, waist-gunner Mark Kasprowicz, has a gash on his forehead from some flying metal. It was amazing that so many of those who had left England almost twelve hours ago had survived. They had been through Hell. Two days later they made their back to Norfolk ready to take up the fight once more.

For their bravery on the mission and their success in causing great damage to the ME109 factory there are many medals awarded on their return to England, but not one for Frank who said he was only doing his duty anyway. He feels very proud of those men who were awarded some recognition for their actions.

Seven days later he is promoted to 1st Lt. To realise how many men have been lost or seriously wounded does take away some of his pleasure though and he suffers from the guilt complex of why them and not me? He knew many of these men, officers and enlisted men, and was proud to be among their number.

The results of the combined raids start to be made known. They have lost 60 B-17s, which means at first glance six hundred men; however, of these men 109 have been killed and 392 are in Prisoner-of War camps. Some have been interned in Switzerland and 60 rescued from the sea and returned to their base. The 100th from Thorpe Abbotts have suffered the most on the Regensburg mission with 9 out of 21 planes sent being shot down, 17 men killed and 59 taken prisoner. The American base officers have made ludicrous claims of having shot down 288 fighters, when the real number would have been in the twenties.

They don't have any big missions to go on for a few days, just practices as the CO believes they can and must improve their formation flying. For relaxation many of the men go to see the latest "Road" film with Bob Hope, Bing Crosby and Dorothy Lamour starring. They laugh at Hope's wisecracks, sing along with Crosby's crooning, but most of their attention of course is on Dorothy Lamour in her skirt, seemingly made of grass, which gives plenty of views of her gorgeous legs. They whistle loudly at her provocative movements and think how they would love to be in her company and what they could do with her given half a chance.

They go back to their Nissen hut with Frank saying she isn't too bad, but Helga's better.

"How can you still be in love with a Kraut when they are knocking so many of our guys out of the skies? Have you seen the shape of some of our boys who have survived when they come back in, legs broken, arms smashed . . . need I go on?"

"I know all this," Frank answers," but can you honestly think that the sweet, gentle girl I knew four years ago has anything to do with this or, bears any responsibility?"

This argument goes on for some time with all discussion of the merits of the beautiful Lamour long since forgotten. Some of the men think that there is logic in Frank's argument, but many are of the opinion, strongly held, that the only good Kraut is a dead one. Co-pilot Gerry Jackson tells them all that it is time to get to sleep

"Knock it off, you guys, let's get some shut-eye; we never know what tomorrow may bring." They all heed his wise words, but if only they knew what the next day would bring.

13

FEARS FOR HELGA

At 06.30 on one chilly October morning an orderly taps certain flyers on the shoulder to inform them that they are flying that day. They then discover that the mission has been delayed for a few hours, as there is a heavy mist over the continent. They take breakfast and then even have time for an early lunch, so they are left guessing with all kinds of possibilities. How they would love a "milk run" for a change, with some relatively easy target in northern France or even Belgium. All this waiting around adds to the tension and there are signs of short tempers amongst some of the men as they argue about stupid, trivial matters.

At last the signal is given them to go to the Ops. Room. Before they are given their target the most astute of them realise that there is "something big" on as there is even a Brigadier General, a one-star man, on the platform. They are told that the Luftwaffe has been trying to bomb their airfields with a large force. "Let's make these bastards pay for this, men! They don't do this to us boys of the Eighth," says the CO in strident terms which none of them remember hearing him use before.

Frank agrees with his fighting talk, but as with all the others he needs to know where they are going. The CO then hands over to Brigadier Harvey — "Ah, that's why he is here!" — who tells them in a calm, measured voice, unlike the aggressive tones of the CO, that there is so much importance attached to their mission later that day that it has been given an ME rating, Maximum Effort. So much for the Milk Run. But yes, where are we going?

The Brigadier is an impressive looking man with a very square jaw and thick, dark-brown hair with an immaculate parting. His uniform jacket has a chestful of campaign ribbons and decorations.

"Major, will you show these boys where they are off to?"

There is a deathly hush as the Group Ops. takes over. Major Rhodes pulls back the curtain. They see the huge map with route marked in red cotton — BREMEN! This is a very heavily defended area with a great concentration of flak batteries. Frank lets out an audible gasp "Something bothering you, Lootenant?" asks the Major.

"No sir. I just wasn't expecting it for some reason."

"Where would you like to have gone instead?"

"Stateside, sir."

There was laughter round the room which helped to ease the tension.

Frank finds it hard to believe that he is going to help bring destruction on this beautiful city that he had grown so fond of. Above all, what about Helga? Of course she has no idea of what he is doing as all communication between them ceased even before the USA entered the war. The last time that they had written to each other Helga had told him that her law studies were going well and he had not written about his work at IG Farben too much, but more about his social life and telling her how much he was missing her. There was heavy censorship then as he could not speak about his work and she could not make any comment on life in the Third Reich. What was she doing? What about her family? What impact was the war making on them? How much impact would his being part of this huge raid have on them? A silly question really as it was bound to have had a great effect in the docks, a major target.

In something like a feeling of numbness they are told of the importance: the huge Focke—Wulf factory—it will be good to give that a going-over—the dockyards with their submarine facilities and repair shops. The Atlas Werke Shipbuilding Company and Bremer Vulkan shipyard were vital to the enemy's naval campaigns. Vegesack, up the River Weser from Bremen, nearer the sea, would also be receiving attention from this ME, as it too had very important U-Boat and dock installations.

They were then given the customary routine of weather conditions, codes, flight formations and routes for each group. Frank's group was to fly north-east over the North Sea and then it was to approach the target from the north-west angle. By now they had some new crew members to replace injured colleagues, luckily none had yet died.

Sgt. Kasprowicz had gone already, injured, and had been followed by Sgt. Speer, Sgt. Bridges and Lt. Harry Schultz, pilot. Harry had gone through battle fatigue, as he was on the edge of cracking up, the others through injuries which would soon be patched up. The new crew had hardly had time to get to know each other and yet here they were together on a mission of this importance where mutual trust and teamwork were so important.

There are three groups and they assemble over the North Sea at Splasher Six. Frank's group is preceded by those marvellous multi-purpose De Havilland Mosquitoes which will drop a device known to hamper enemy radar used for their flak.

It is a perfect October day and the timing with meeting the other groups has been exactly as planned. There is a certain amount of gunfire as they cross the coast but nothing compared with what could come. They have been told that Bremen has very strong flak defences, but surprisingly few fighter air fields. Approaching Bremen, they realise how much more intensive is the flak. The chatter on the radio within the plane is becoming more and more excitable.

"Did you see that Fort get hit? Tail plane gone. At least four guys have managed to bale out." That's John Jameson, the new waist gunner.

A stern rebuke follows from the skipper, Jim Broad. "Keep your eye on the job, Jameson. This isn't a ball game — we don't need a running commentary, thank you."

It is impossible to stay quiet with all the surrounding action. More and more Forts are being hit, some shot down, the majority damaged in various degrees.

"Bogeys at three o'clock, two FWs, coming straight at us."

"There goes that new crew. Caught a flak burst on the port engine. Crew baling out — can see at least six of them."

The tight groupings so necessary for defensive cover are now being dispersed with the ferocity of the flak and the persistence of the German fighters.

There are so many men attempting to parachute from stricken planes that Larry Gomes, the Bombardier and crew wit, comments:" The general told us it was a bombing raid, now I see it is an airborne invasion. We ain't had no training for that."

Still the battle goes on as the Forts make for their targets. Frank's plane drops its load of twelve 500 pound bombs causing the plane to shudder as it loses all this weight. To their right they see a B-17 with two engines on fire start to dive but nobody is leaving it. This is a tactic whereby a plane with damaged engines can dive very quickly and with luck the flames will die out. They haven't time to see if this move is successful as they are not out of the mire themselves. Many of these bombs will have dropped on not only Bremen, but surrounding towns such as Lilienthal, Ganderksee or Delmenhorst! Will that lino factory or that tower still be there?

When not at the gun he is writing down furiously details such as time, place and altitude of flak, of rocket bursts, of enemy aircraft shot down, of colleagues hit by flak or fighters. He is too busy to feel any fear and acts as though an automaton. A Messerschmitt flies past them so close that they can clearly see the pilot's face. How strange can one's thoughts be in such a situation. Frank has seen an enemy almost face-to-face who is trying to kill him and his comrades. Yet the thought comes to him wondering about this man, Bernhardt or Fritz, who also has a family and is flesh and blood. He too is putting his life on the line and is probably a very pleasant person in different circumstances, likes a drink, plays sport, has a steady girlfriend somewhere in Germany and so on. If she is anything like his German girl, then she is something very special. Just how crazy is war!

It's time to banish all these thoughts from his mind and navigate the plane back home. He realises from the anguished cries that some of the crew have been hit. Waist—gunner Ken Jackson in such a vulnerable spot with the side wide open is shouting in pain as he has been hit in the face by flying shrapnel and needs morphine. There is blood flowing from the wound. Rear—Gunner Mitchell Hanks is suffering from oxygen deprivation as his apparatus has been hit by a bullet. Hanks needs the plane to descend rapidly to below the oxygen level. As his fellow gunner goes to Jackson's aid, he has to wade through a sea of spent cartridges. The sky around them is full of bits of planes, flying debris everywhere: tail fins, parts of engines, sections of wings, American and German. At times this can seem as dangerous as the flak or the bogeys.

They start to descend, expecting to be chased by the ME 109s, but miraculously there are none. On the way home they may have to be challenged by the notorious "Abbeville Kids," those notorious Luftwaffe fighter pilots stationed in northern France.

As they straighten out, however, they are spotted by a pair of German fighters. They attack and seriously damage the starboard engine but there is the consolation of Hank Crosby in the upper turret shooting down one of their pursuers. The engine power has been severely diminished as they limp home, but fortunately there are no further enemy fighters chasing them. The sky is clear of all planes as they cross the coast over The Netherlands. They are losing engine power and height but just make it close to their base to land at Framlingham where they skid to a halt on the runway finishing up with a ninety-degree turn. The fire-tenders are quickly out but are not needed. All pay credit to the great skill of Jim Broad.

The whole mission has cost the Eighth Force thirty bombers, that is three hundred men. On de-briefing they are congratulated for their great courage and accuracy under heavy flak and determined fighter opposition. Several days later they learn that they have been recommended for a Distinguished Unit Citation; not only that, but Frank and Jim Broad have been awarded the DSO for leadership and courage "Above and beyond the call of duty."

They are very proud but don't think too much of this daylight policy or of the propaganda about the Norden bombsight—"A mighty large pickle barrel must have been used in the testing?" opines Wally

Cipriani. The experiences the men are undergoing are beginning to have a great effect on them, emotionally and physically, much of it relieved by gallows humour, such as joking about baling out and being a POW, where at least there wouldn't be this daily fear of some horrible death in the skies. One of them wonders whether before a flight you are likely to suffer constipation or dysentery.

"My God, you're an optimist!" states Wally Thorne, the bombardier from Ohio, in reply to the possibility of becoming a German prisoner.

They are suffering greatly from all these missions. There is the knotting of the stomach before the flight, the naked fear as soon as the flak begins and the fighters appear to hunt them down. To have a successful run-in to bomb successfully the pilot has to keep at a steady height, at a steady speed which gives the flak a far easier target. Contrary to orders, many planes trying to avoid the anti-aircraft barrage drop their load whilst weaving out of the way. The conditions inside the plane are cramped and give the feeling of claustrophobia; there is the worry over the oxygen equipment which if damaged, causes men to die. Flying in the bitter cold so many degrees below freezing causes malfunction of essential parts, such as gun-sights and bomb bay doors and leads to the windows icing up. Waist gunners at open windows with freezing winds were more exposed than the rest of the crew. Frost bite was a serious cause of injury, more even than enemy action. Men could lose their fingers and thus have to be discharged. The electric suits they wore were not always dependable as they could short and give electric shocks. There were men in the plane who were badly injured, crying in pain with nobody else in the plane having enough medical knowledge to cope properly. The atmosphere was fetid with the smell of stale sweat, urine and cordite and the remains of cigarette smoke from just before take-off. Basic needs of nature, such as urinating were impossible to do hygienically and men had to wet their clothing. There was the aftermath in the effect on the men psychologically. How difficult it was to banish from their minds what they had seen and experienced such as B-I7s being shot to pieces, their colleagues' bodies mutilated, parachutes not opening and the grisly sights on returning to base. When an injured Fort landed after being badly damaged, the fire tenders and First-Aid vehicles would be on the scene immediately taking out badly injured and men so burned they were disfigured. Even worse was when they had to hose out the remains of some unfortunate who had been directly hit by a shell. Most of the men have some kind of superstition which they unfailingly try to adhere to. There are those who won't shave on the day of a mission, or those who insist on being the fourth to climb into the plane. Many of them carry good luck charms, such as necklaces, bracelets, family photographs in the left-hand pocket and there was one who even had elastic bands round his wrists.

There was also the nightmare of returning to your room and finding that the beds had been prepared for the next incumbents as the previous occupier had been killed or parachuted into captivity. There would be no trace of him as all photographs and personal effects were immediately stored for transport home to the States. It was difficult to grow too close with your colleagues as their death would be too distressing. On the other hand, some of them take the attitude of making the most of their time, live while you can: get drunk, make friends with the local girls or see the countryside. Being so far from home, made many of them lose their inhibitions and so they felt free to go and see whom they wanted without mothers, grandmothers or, in some cases, even wives and girlfriends, not knowing what exactly they were up to.

All this was a very serious problem, causing psychologists to be appointed at each base. There had been an all-too-clear negative effect on morale— yet still the ideological pursuit of bombing by day continued. Every man's goal and ambition was to reach the magical target of twenty-five missions, enough to discharge you from bombing raids. As if in consolation for all their efforts and sacrifices, the 318st Bombardment Group is awarded a Distinguished Unit Citation. The grim truth, however, is that thirty planes have been lost, and of greater importance that means three hundred men. Where can they continue to find and train crews of such calibre as replacements?

Frank feels that if he were to survive, he would have the basis for writing a critical book on his experiences. However, he mustn't brood too much; there is still a war to be won.

14

SOCIAL LIFE IN NORFOLK

As the days pass, they realise just what an attraction they are to the local population. This has been a quiet part of the country since time immemorial and the presence of all these foreigners with their giant, exciting B-17s is incredibly interesting. The roads near the airfield are often filled with the fascinated natives from far and wide; indeed, one of the roads is almost on a runway. The young boys and girls are absolutely thrilled at seeing these huge, yet beautiful bombers with the roundel of the white American five-pointed star on a blue background on the fuselage and on the wings. The tail-plane is high off the ground and they love to watch the way in which the crew so athletically pull themselves up into the body of the aircraft and to listen to the accents of the airmen and ground staff. They sound just like Hollywood film stars and have a glamour, even aura, about them. The young females are particularly struck by them. The Americans play on this and "talk big" about their large homes back in the States, their close friendship with American movie stars and even claim to be one of them. They soon become known as GIs or, not quite as affectionately, Yanks.

From time to time the GIs have dances in the camp, usually in one of the big hangars with a giant B-17 in the background. As well as all the locals, girls, not necessarily all teenagers or in their early twenties, are brought in by bus from a wide area. They love the Glenn Miller style of music with "Moonlight Serenade" and "In the Mood" being especially popular. What really thrills the girls though is the new style of dancing the Americans have introduced: the jitterbug. In this the girls are thrown over the men's shoulders and between their legs, all done in very quick tempo and most energetic. They all find it so exhilarating, a wonderful release from flying or a dreary office job. The atmosphere is electric with many of the men climbing on to the wings of the Fort, or even sitting on the beams overhead.

At one of the dances there is a slight lull which allows one of the sergeants in the ground crew who sees himself as an up-and-coming Frank Sinatra take the stage. At first there are good-natured jeers and whistles which lead the MC, a stocky warrant officer, to ask the men to give him a chance. The jeers soon to cheers as he sings "Smoke Gets In Your Eyes," the Jerome Kern classic. He is given a great reception and draws further cheers when he remarks how appropriate this song is in the unhealthy, smoke-filled hangar. The pleadings for an encore are turned down by the MC who says that the band is the priority, but it could be possible to hear him at a later date.

Frank does not exactly shine at this new dance, but does find it a most helpful way of forgetting the worries of being in the air. The girls who come have done everything they can to make themselves attractive and the great majority have succeeded. Naturally many couples slip off to somewhere more private for further entertainment. Whilst all this is taking place, there are crews preparing to take off at dawn the following day to attack some target in the Reich.

The mighty roar of the B-17s' engines warming up for take-off before manoeuvring into position inspires awe in the villagers. The youngsters, boys and girls, instead of collecting car numbers, take to noting the plane numbers and everybody is fascinated by the artwork on the front of the fuselage. Girls in various forms of undress are particular favourites, but then there are place names, family or girl friends' names and even esoteric quotes. It is a stirring sight to see the planes climb into the sky with ever-decreasing size as they set off for some enemy target. There is just as much excitement when they return hours later in usually diminished numbers.

The area around Diss, the village near their base, seems to have almost been caught in a time warp. The boys from the big cities find it hard to believe just how slow the life is away from the base and out into the country, even though it is difficult to find somewhere too far from a US airfield. The land is very flat and although there is beautiful scenery, it is not quite the same without the odd hill or mountain to break it up.

The men soon realise that the best way to get around is to beg, borrow or, in extreme circumstances, steal a bike. The flat countryside makes cycling easy. In the summer it is very refreshing and enjoyable to get away from it all and cycle down the picturesque lanes, riding past old-fashioned pubs, looking at beautiful country houses with their lovely gardens. There are quaint cottages with their thatched roofs, they can listen to the birds, or look at the flowers and trees with no flak or MEs to bother about. It doesn't take them too long to realise that in the fields there is a very interesting form of life apart from the horses, sheep and cattle: that is the Land Girls as they are known. As East Anglia is a very rural community, these ladies, some volunteers, others conscripted from all walks of life, are vital to help feed the country with most of the men away fighting. Although this is true, their agricultural necessity is not the first thought on the Americans' minds and they start to take a further interest in the countryside.

They have a mixed reception from the locals, as some resent their arrival at upsetting the sleepy village life and bringing the area into the twentieth century; others, especially the schoolboys and girls, are thrilled at the excitement they bring. There are more of the villagers who favour them but all realise their importance. Whatever the feeling, all agree that they have made a tremendous impact on the area.

There were problems when they first came over as this was a totally new way of life to sleepy East Anglia. They drove on the wrong side of the road, could be loud and brash and whistled at all the girls they saw. The countryside was a mass of khaki and vehicles which were trying to use unsuitable, narrow roads not fit for purpose. Imagine all these lively young men dropping in on a peaceful countryside of fields lined with trees and hedgerows and chocolate box villages and cottages. The town of Lavenham for instance was a beautiful place to visit with its old houses of half-timbered cottages.

They love going into the pubs, a way of life they have not experienced before. Just as a way of ridding themselves of the base atmosphere, they happily drink pints of lukewarm ale. Before long their extrovert characters cause a thaw in the more reserved locals and they drink together happily, for the most part. There is a mutual interest in each other's way of life and before long the Americans join groups of locals, not keeping to a strict segregation. They are generous with their cigarettes, the famous Camel. The locals love to hear their songs and if there is a piano in the pub, there always seems to be an American who can perform on it; Glenn Miller tunes go down particularly well.

The men from Thorpe Abbotts find these English pubs so quaint, so different from those back home. There are the brasses all around the walls, kept highly polished, the low oak beams, the leaded windows, the stone fire place, a most welcome feature for most of the year as a retreat from their less than warm Nissen huts. The locals appear to have their own set spots, it seems at times hereditary and they are jealously guarded. There was almost a diplomatic incident when a young sergeant dared to sit in old Ken Brandish's spot in the corner to the merriment of the locals.

"My God, young lad, you be a brav'un to do that. It's been his spot since nineteen-twenty, and his father's afore 'im. I think 'e just be gone to relieve 'isself at the toilet; two pints be enough for him, even though he prides 'isself on being an 'ard drinker" This was from the ruddy-faced landlord, Henry

Armitage, who had run the Swan with his wife Bessy for the last sixteen years.

The youngster, an innocent twenty-year old lad from Detroit, duly apologises and receives a reluctant acceptance from old Ken when he returns minutes later. Harmony restored and the offending party re-seated, all returned to the business of the evening with Ken being bought a pint of best ale to soothe his troubled feelings.

The low beams, whilst adding so much to the atmosphere, were something of a handicap to the taller Americans. Frank, who was about 6"1', had great trouble initially in avoiding them and had a few cracks on the head before learning how to bend just at the right moment. The first time he ducked under successfully he earned a round of good-natured applause and, as a bonus, a drink on the house

Frank and his friends find their encounters with the villagers a great source of material for letters home, escaping talking about the war. The married men have to be a little more discreet in relating what social life they have!

The shopkeepers are certainly pleased as their pay is so much better than the wages of the locals and although they can buy most of what they want in their PX store, they are still regular customers in the shops. On the other hand, their money causes much jealousy when it is compared with that given to British servicemen. Young men cannot compete with them when it comes to impressing women and fights have not been unknown. Their generosity is looked upon cynically by many, particularly when they bring presents of ham or chocolates to the mothers of attractive girls, cigarettes to the fathers or silk stockings for the females in the family.

Young boys think they are amazing, glamorous, generous and friendly. The expression "Any gum, chum?" becomes part of the language and the airmen rarely disappoint the youngsters.

To try and overcome the problems the CO on the base arranges for some of the men to go and talk to the villagers in the local hall. Frank is one of these selected. He is a little nervous at first but soon relaxes when he realises that the mixed assembly is so attentive. He begins by thanking them all for their hospitality to these strangers so far from home. He acknowledges that it must be difficult for them to see their community being taken over by these young men whose accents must be so unfamiliar and ways so alien. He sees many of them nodding their head in agreement and smiling.

He then asks them to understand the viewpoints of the Americans who are so far from home and loved ones. They have not always found it easy, especially when they think of the reason for their being here. On the question of strange accents he then does a very passable imitation of the way in which the Norfolk people speak. There is much laughter at this, more so when he compares it favourably with the Warrington accent up north; he says his audience speak what to American ears is so colourful, but the northern accent was rather dull and dreary." 'Ere, 'ere," came a chorus of East Anglian voices.

Frank feels that he has done a good job in trying to put the American side of it and many of the locals come up to him to shake hands. They say they have appreciated what he and his colleagues are doing. When he returns to the camp he is told that this has been an exercise over a wide area. The news filters through that there has generally been a good response, but in some bases, reports of a slight sense of not quite hostility, but a feeling of being invaded perhaps.

15

LUNCH WITH A LOCAL FAMILY

Frank and his friend Lyndon Rogers, a bombardier from Nebraska, have become very friendly with a butcher from Diss called Jim Anness. He is a mine of information about the area and its inhabitants. He has some funny stories to tell about his customers over the years. He had had a shop there for over thirty years. This was a very settled community and people tended to stay there all their lives, even though some of the younger ones had gone to find their fortune in the "big town" of Norwich. The customers had been very loyal to him and had been the same for many years even before the food rationing began. Jim has very rosy cheeks, something of a Roman nose and is very broad shouldered.

The two airmen love his East Anglian accent which makes them think so much of country folk and an easy, unhurried style of living.

After they have met him a few times in a pub by the Mere, a lovely stretch of water off the River Waveney, and learned much about the history of the town and its characters which he told in that slow, measured manner, he surprises them somewhat. He asks them if they would like to join himself, his wife and teenage son at their home for a Sunday meal when their duties allowed. He understood perfectly that plans could have to be altered at the last moment. It also enters his mind that they may have been injured or even worse by then.

They are extremely grateful for this, with the proviso of course that, as he says, duty could intervene, but they also add what he has just been thinking. As this is now Friday, they think that the following Sunday could be suitable as there have been no rumours of impending action. The boys back at the base are very envious when they are told that this meal is to be at a butcher's home — "No need then for those ration cards that these limeys have to put up with then!"

They arrive at the Anness house at about three o'clock to be met at the door by all the family. Mrs. Anness is a matronly lady about fifty years old. She has blue eyes, a dimpled chin and what is called a roll hairstyle. She is so thrilled to see these two handsome GIs that she is in a bit of a fluster trying to please, embarrassing them and her husband. Mrs. Anness has of course put on her best Sunday frock and is quite embarrassed when the men give her a tin of ham, some chocolates and chewing gum for son Jim. "Oh, you shouldn't have bothered," but her protestations are waved aside.

"Please sit down. No, not in that one, the dog's been sleeping there. Jim, get that other one in the back room."

As if on cue, the dog, an elderly-looking black Labrador, sidles into the room and demands to be patted.

The son is about thirteen and has a sturdy build. He works on the land at a nearby farm during the school holidays and sometimes at odd times during the term. He is called Jim after his father. He is a little shy at first, but Frank and Lyndon soon make him feel at ease. As with all the local boys he is thrilled with the airbase being so close. His accent is a little difficult to follow which is made worse by his excitement. He wants to know all about the Forts and where the airmen have been. Of course, to boys his age it all seems a great adventure; the real experiences of these men are not known to him except when he hears the fire tenders and ambulances racing to the incoming planes and hears the gloomy comments of the seniors. His father asks him to give the men some peace so that he and his mother can get in a word or two.

"I'm sure you lads would like a cup of tea. You do drink it, don't you?" Somehow her accent doesn't seem quite like those they have become accustomed to listening to.

"Thanks, ma'am. No, we are used to coffee in the States, but tea is just fine."

Frank adds to Lyndon's comments by agreeing, "Mrs. Anness, I'm sure that it'll be just right if you've made it."

She blushes a little at this comment and insists that they call her Gladys.

"Well boys, how do you like it here?" Jim asks, even though they have discussed this at the pub, but it gives him a chance to say how the war has changed their scenery and way of life. Not only is there the important factor of the GIs, the airfields and the planes, but things have changed in other ways too. The countryside was suffering in the 30s through poverty and the fields were becoming very neglected. The farmers were struggling, but now the fields have been revived to grow cereal crops and any spare piece of ground has been turned over to grow food. They must have seen all these posters encouraging people to "Dig For Victory."

It's time now for something to eat, so Gladys places them round the table with Frank and Lyndon on either side of her. As Jim is a butcher they have a lovely piece of beef, normally strictly" under the counter" for favoured customers, but these are special guests. There is no shortage of potatoes and vegetables with this being a farming area. For dessert, or pudding, there is fruit crumble and custard. This traditional Sunday meal goes down well with the guests who are certainly not used to this kind of meal at the base. Young Jim, trying to impress the GIs, gives great help in clearing away all the dishes.

"Blimey, can you two come every week?" says Jim snr. with just a touch of sarcasm.

"Oh, leave the boy alone, he's doing his best, Jim." As always, mother comes to his support.

Now they must have a further cup of tea, which the Americans again politely accept. After all, to have the English version of coffee would be far worse. Gladys now far more relaxed as the time passes, asks them questions about America which she has always wanted to know. She hasn't heard all the conversations about the States which Jim has heard in the pub, so needs to know more about American life. She had been so busy in the kitchen that she hadn't been able to join in the chat.

"What is the situation regarding Negroes, for instance? I realise that you two boys aren't from the southern states, so what is going on?" This is a very surprising question as they had no idea that someone in sleepy Norfolk would have any idea about American states, let alone where they were.

"Well Gladys, they are supposed to be protected by the law, but I'm not too sure this is totally accepted in the former slave states? What do you think, Frank?"

"I'm afraid that I have to agree with you on that one, Lyndon. There is much discrimination even in the forces when you could expect some kind of unity, but there again the sores run deep after the way some of our guys treated them. Some of those southern bigots even resent their speaking to white girls. The situation seemed to be bad round Burtonwood up in northern England from what we hear and fights were not uncommon."

"We have seen some real rough and tumbles round here. Often it's been because of women, but often we have noticed those on the ground not wanting to work with black people—a disgrace, I think," says Gladys emphatically.

The Americans are surprised and pleased to hear this liberal view in Norfolk. However, as the conversation develops, Frank and Lyndon become more and more impressed with the knowledge of their hostess. She asks them about such things as President Roosevelt's New Deal and America's problems after the Wall St. crash. It seems at times that she knows more than they did.

Jim is glowing with pride at this demonstration of her intelligence." I'm amazed she stuck wi' me all these years. She be far too bright."

"Don't be so silly, Jim. You're no fool."

Before long, all is revealed. Gladys comes from a fairly prosperous part of Sussex and was set to train as a teacher. She had come as a teenager with some of her girl-friends on a country holiday to Norfolk. After a few days they went to a fair near Norwich where she met Jim with some lads. She was a little shy but was won over by his ready wit and, she must admit, flattery. When she returned home they exchanged letters. He wrote in such a sincere, if at times ungrammatical, way, that she felt she had to see him again. Her parents weren't too happy, as he didn't seem "good enough" for their precious daughter. She went up to Norfolk again as soon as she could, stayed with one of Jim's relatives and decided he was for her They married two years later and they both say that they haven't regretted a minute of it.

This naturally leads on to romantic lives of the two Americans. Lyndon has a girl-friend back home in Nebraska with whom he corresponds regularly, but as yet there is no wedding in the offing. This discussion leads to Frank's recalling all his memories of the beautiful Helga. Jim, and especially Gladys, are so sympathetic to him in his plight and feel for him for having to go on raids so near her home town.

Bringing Helga in to the conversation has made him so nostalgic just when he though he had rid himself of memories of being unfaithful to her. But for how long can he keep these memories of her alive when there seems little likelihood of ever meeting her again and he has no idea of what has happened to her? Is he being too hard on himself?

The time has just seemed to go past with indecent speed and it is time to depart. They have had such a wonderful Sunday and duty calls—who knows where this time? Jim and Gladys say they must come again and the boys agree wholeheartedly.

16

LIFE IN GERMANY 1939-43

Whilst Frank was totally involved in the war effort, he often thought of Helga and wondered what she was doing. How was the war affecting her? He still had so many happy memories of their time together. In her turn, she thought a good deal about him and could not come to terms with the fact that they were enemies whose families, friends and colleagues were actually trying to kill each other. Did he ever think about her? It was so obvious that war was about to break out as 1939 advanced.

The inevitable came on September 1st 1939 as Germany invaded Poland. All the propaganda inspired by Goebbels had worked on the vast majority and there was euphoria as after concessions wrung out of Great Britain over Czechoslovakia and the Anschluss of Austria, there was no stopping the mighty Third Reich in its ambitions to extend its territories in searching for Lebensraum. The Jews and Slavs needed to be put in their place and soon the glorious Führer's empire would extend in ever—increasing momentum.

The atmosphere in Delmenhorst is one of fairly subdued satisfaction, but in Bremen as the news comes out in booming announcements over the loudspeakers and repeated radio bulletins, there is almost a holiday feeling. On the way into the city Helga was very uneasy and Herr Wassermann had reservations which he did not air to anybody but his wife and daughter; his son was not brought into his confidence because of his enthusiasm for the Nazis.

Helga had not yet finished her law studies, but wondered what the future held for her. Would she be able to carry on in the usual manner upon successfully graduating and being accepted by a legal practice to gain experience? She felt uncertain about her future, especially as she was sure that the United States wouldn't be too long before joining Great Britain and France; she couldn't imagine Frank being an enemy. Her parents had in fact persuaded her to suspend her course in Hamburg as they were fearful of the heavy bombing there. Bremen was also suffering, but at least she would be near to them. In addition the journey between the two cities was becoming more and more difficult with all the wartime transport problems when she felt like a weekend at home. She had agreed to attend a further education college in Bremen to follow a law course there, not of as high a standard as at Hamburg but enough to keep her focussed.

Her father had now become busier than ever in his work in the dockyards. The U-Boats were being refitted and prepared for Atlantic duty twenty-four hours a day and new ships were being launched continually. He was responsible for about fifty men and had been moved from the city to nearby Vegesack.

Frau Wassermann was a hard working Hausfrau who has not been taken in by the Nazi ideology, but was careful not to let her feelings known. Her son annoyed her in his aggressive attitude towards Germany's enemies and the Jews. Karl had been thoroughly indoctrinated at school and at the Hitler Youth meetings he attended so enthusiastically. He alarmed his parents when he came home one evening and said that he knew of a family whose son had reported his father to the police for saying that the Jewish persecution was inhumane. "What happened then?" asked Frau Wassermann in what she hoped was a calm voice.

"Oh, he was visited by two plain-clothes policemen who lectured him in a very threatening manner."

Barry RICKSON

The first two years of the war had been surprisingly good as far as food was concerned. Hitler had been careful not to be too stringent with issuing limitations on food for the German people as this could have an adverse effect on morale. There was rationing, but Germany had been sustained by plundering from defeated countries; however, once Operation Barbarossa, the invasion of Russia, was proving more difficult than had been anticipated, there was an immediate reduction in the meat allowance from 500 grams per person to 400 grams and then there were further cuts. There was a tiered system of allowances depending on the nature of the work involved. Herr Wassermann was on the highest allowance as his work was considered to be physically demanding. The rest of the family were on a lower allowance, sufficient to live on, but not allowing any luxuries. The allied control of the seas prevented many goods from reaching the country. They missed coffee and had to make do with a substitute known as Ersatz which was just about drinkable. To buy food there was a system of ration cards with Essensmarken, similar to points in the UK, when the shopkeeper had to denote the number of units spent. This was a bureaucratic nightmare for them.

There had been a serious problem at the beginning of 1940 when the intense cold caused many of one of Germany's main arteries, that is the

122

rivers, to freeze up. This had caused great difficulties with the transportation of food and other vital supplies. The River Weser had been no exception and the Bremen district was seriously affected.

Vegetables and local fruits were not rationed and if you happened to live near the country and friendly farmers, you were better off than those who lived in the city. Herr Wassermann could at times bring home clandestinely from the docks some useful metal or tools which could be exchanged for food with a friendly farmer. For others in rural areas rabbit was becoming almost a staple diet. As the war developed and Frank and his colleagues together with the RAF were bombing their cities, the food supplies were being reduced. It took all Frau Wassermann's ingenuity to provide daily meals. The German advance into Russia was being turned into a "strategic withdrawal" on all fronts and there was the disaster at Stalingrad where so many soldiers of the Wehrmacht had been lost.

Herr Wassermann's workload had increased substantially with so many U-Boats being damaged, new ones being constructed and then there was the bombing! Since America entered the war, Bremen had suffered dreadfully with the Americans bombing by day and the RAF by night. It had been a dreadful time for all of the family, but especially Klaus. There were so many days when he wondered if he would ever return home in one piece. Margrit could not relax until she heard his key in the door. Delmenhorst did not suffer greatly from the persistent bombing, even though so close to the big city.

Helga was caught in Bremen one day in October 1943 near the main station when she heard the sirens wail and saw the vapour trails of the Flying Fortresses at a great height. The flak batteries ringing the city were in full action and could be heard and with their shells bursting in the clear sky made a great impression on Helga, sights and sounds which she would never forget. There was chaos with people dashing everywhere, children being lost and the elderly not knowing what to do or where to go. She raced to a large underground shelter and went to sit on a bench with a young mother and her two children. The lady had blond plaits wound round her head and soon started to breast-feed her youngster, a daughter. It turned out that her two brothers were in the army, one in Russia and the other as quite a contrast in Guernsey, one of the Channel Isles. They had not heard from Manfred for some time but they knew that at least he had not been at Stalingrad and was due for leave. Every family seemed to have a relative, friend or acquaintance who had been killed or badly wounded on the Russian Front. Stalingrad in particular had been portrayed as a strategic withdrawal by the Goebbels ministry, but the trains continually coming home from Russia piled with wounded or dead soldiers told a different story.

The conversation in the shelter was about food rationing, relatives in the armed forces and the bombing. As there were bound to be informers down there, nobody could be critical about the state of affairs, but how Helga wished she could say something. She kept quiet as she did not want to face interrogation for criticising the leadership and consequently being sent to a police cell. The atmosphere was rancid with the smell of sweaty bodies on this rather warm October day. Although the bombing was directed at the docks, some stray ones landed nearby and shook the foundations of the shelter, deep as it was.

An elderly man, who was unable to take it much longer, screeched out, "Das ist Wahnsinn!" To accuse the leaders of madness was a treasonable offence and not surprisingly he was confronted by a tall, sinister figure, wearing a long overcoat and a trilby which half-hid his face. When he discovered that the man was sixty years old and had fought on the Somme, he released him with a severe warning.

A prime example of the danger of speaking out occurred in Munich when Sophie Scholl and her brother Hans, students at Munich University and founders of the White Rose League, were caught handing out anti-Nazi documents and were guillotined on the judgement of the dreaded Roland

Freisler in February 1943. Sophie's dying words were "Es lebe die Freiheit!" or "Long Live Freedom!" Many of the other students involved were caught later and also executed. It is no wonder that people were frightened of criticising the government.

At last they heard the All-Clear sirens and trooped out of the shelter, weary and dazed. There was devastation everywhere, a scene of great destruction, office blocks collapsed, trams ripped apart, ambulances and fire engines working at full speed, and bodies of people who had not been quick enough to make for the shelter were strewn over the pavements.

Although the least likely of people to be aggressive, Helga made up her mind after this first-hand experience of seeing her fellow Germans killed, injured and terrified, that she was going to play her part in helping her country. She had not been an enthusiastic member of the Bund Deutscher Mädel, the girls' equivalent of the Hitler Youth, but had been able to leave at eighteen years of age. The destruction of her beloved city was beginning to make her see things rather differently.

She had had several friendships with young men, mostly university students, but nothing really serious, just casual relationships. She was quite keen on a smart Panzer officer, but he had disappeared to Libya as part of the Afrika Korps. She still often thought, however, of the handsome young American who had made such an impact on her life in his brief stay in her country; she had this strange feeling of wanting to stay faithful to him; she wondered if he thought the same about her, even though they were at war.

Karl was still very enthusiastic about his country's anti-Bolshevik campaign but after he had seen some disgraceful treatment of young Jewish mothers and elderly people he was less enthusiastic about their persecution. He was maturing and the thought of some of these Nazi thugs, young and middle-aged, treating these helpless people in such a way brought out his latent feelings of humanity. He was still in the Hitler youth as he had to be. If a young boy left without a good reason or refused to join, his father could lose his job. He was now becoming interested in girls and had had one or two dates with Melanie, a fair-haired girl in the Bund Deutscher Mädel. She enjoyed the outdoor life involved and didn't have any interest in the politics, but was smart enough not to make this obvious. Without saying too much, his parents thought that she was helping him to mature.

17

STUTTGART AND KIEL
NIGHTMARES

It is now December 1943 and although the Allies are getting on top, the RAF and the USAAF are suffering terrible losses of men and aircraft. Frank and his ever-changing colleagues are beginning to question the statistics and figures given out by the intelligence reports. Have they really shot down all those enemy fighters? Figures can be distorted here as in the heat of battle several gunners could claim the same aircraft. As for the destruction done to German industry, they have never stayed too long over the target to judge for themselves and the photo interpreters cannot be as certain as they claim to be. No, the Nazis may not be the only ones with a highly efficient propaganda organisation. There have been two frighteningly disastrous raids to Schweinfurt in August and October when the USAAF lost well over one hundred bombers, the lack of long-distance fighter escorts being a crucially telling factor.

In between these calamitous raids to Schweinfurt there is yet another day of gloom. After the Regensburg/Schweinfurt raids, in September there is an ill-conceived plan to attack the ball-bearing plant at Stuttgart, deep in German territory in Baden-Wurttemberg. The weather over the target is appalling with heavy cloud formations, which the met. experts should have been more aware of. The B-17s circle the city with no idea of where to bomb. Over two hundred, about two-thirds of the original number, return home with full bomb loads. After so much fuel being wasted over the target, the decision is made by many crews to jettison their bombs at random, otherwise this excess weight would make it nearly impossible to return home. This they do, including Frank's. He is fuming for several reasons: the waste of fuel and bombs; the incompetence of the leaders back at base and the unnecessary loss of life on the ground of innocent people — he never has been a believer in the philosophy that the only good German is a dead one — but above all, he thinks of all those young airmen's lives sacrificed so needlessly, perhaps to satisfy some senior officer's ego.

On the way back many planes have to ditch in the English Channel after their fuel had run out. Luckily they are close to England, so most are rescued by British launches. Frank's plane is one of those which has had to come down "in the drink." His crew is rescued by a launch from Folkestone in Kent. These sailors have shown remarkable courage and dedication in finding them and then bringing them to safety. On return to base he discovers that they have lost over forty Forts, plus four hundred men, on a mission that should never have been. Over seventy Fortresses had aborted when learning of the weather conditions. He vows that if he is ever given a job in Ops., he would try to prevent this kind of fiasco ever happening again.

As the war is intensifying, Frank is finding that his missions are becoming more and more strenuous as the magic number of twenty-five is growing closer. He is now a veteran of fourteen raids over enemy territory to places such as St. Nazaire, Bremen, Regensburg, Wilhelmshaven, Leipzig, Stuttgart, Kiel and Brunswick.

One that was to stand out in his memory is the raid to Kiel in northern Germany later in December 1943. Apart from the damage done to that mighty naval base on the Baltic, it was significant for the fact that for the first time they were escorted there and back by the updated version of the Mustang or P-51. It had added petrol tanks which added to its range and was to prove an incredible help in winning the war in the air. If they were to continue to bomb by day, it was reassuring to know that you had these excellent fighters with you to hold off the Bogeys.

The flak approaching this great port was predictable in its intensity. Two of Frank's group had been shot down over Denmark; he had not even had time to learn the names of the crews. Coming in at low level over Kiel Bay to attack the shipping had been a nightmare with intense flak for the leaders. Those due to come in behind abandoned the low-level approach and from a theoretically safer height bombed the city, a form of "area bombing" which the Americans had tried to avoid. At least two of the Forts were seen to come down into the icy waters of the harbour.

Frank's crew is one of the lucky ones as very badly hit with one engine severely damaged and the rudder half-shot away, they had just about reached their home base, thanks to the superb skills of the pilot, Lt. Brian Kennedy from Michigan. On their return they learn that nine of the group had been shot down over Europe and another two had been so badly damaged that they had come down in the North Sea. Three were so far unaccounted for and the officers in the control tower are scouring the skies with binoculars to watch out optimistically for their arrival.

There is a loud cry from the station commander as one is seen in the distance limping home. As it approaches, the red emergency flares are released from the plane. The ambulance and fire tender are immediately called for and race to the runway. Unfortunately, it doesn't arrive there as several hundred yards away it explodes and showers engines, wings, metal and bodies over the earth. It was a daily occurrence perhaps over East Anglia, but still a sight which is impossible to get over. Now there are so many more letters for the chaplain and CO to write and so many more dreadful memories. How can one describe these things to parents and loved ones back home?

Just before these raids there was an incident which upset the hierarchy as a gross breach of military discipline, but as it didn't end in loss of life amused the others and was a talking point for a while. Lt. Alan Jones, an experienced pilot and something of a ladies' man, decided to go on a joyride with three land girls. His pretext was that he was testing one of the engines, but in reality he was trying to impress one of them in particular, a redhead from Kent whom he had spotted when on a cycle ride in the country. Unfortunately the plane never got off the ground, swerved off the runway, hit a tree, lost one of the engines and most of a wing before crashing into another tree and finally coming to a halt in a farmyard after smashing a barn and several other buildings. Miraculously nobody was injured, but he never saw the redhead again! He was court martialled, fined $150 and had an extra mission added to his quota.

The thought of writing letters to the States gives Frank a feeling of guilt, as he has not replied to his parents' most recent one. In the evening he writes home and, as usual, tries to avoid causing them any worry. He casually mentions that he has been on missions, but gives no indication of the dangers he and his colleagues have faced. He writes again of the countryside and the people he has met, especially the Anness family. He tells them about Lyndon Rogers, his drinking buddy. He briefly mentions an incident between racial groups. The recent American Presidential election was alluded to as both his parents were now keen Democrats and supported Franklin D Roosevelt in his battle with Republican Thomas E Dewey, Governor of New York. FDR won for an unprecedented fourth term.

Frank and Lyndon have recently been to Norwich to look around before going to enjoy a meal and drink. Whilst they are wandering round, they hear a commotion down a side-street where it is obvious that American servicemen are involved. There fighting going on between white and black airmen. They step in to try to stop the mayhem, their officers' bars doing the trick. The white ones are obviously from the southern states as their accents reveal. The trouble was all because the black soldiers had the effrontery to approach local girls and talk to them, and in some cases even put their arms round them. Frank hadn't quite realised just how liberal he was as he tears into the white soldiers.

"Don't you guys realise we are fighting this war to end this kind of racism? Adolf would just love to hear about this going on over here in England. I'm absolutely ashamed of you—to think you are supposed to be fellow Americans."

"The lootenant has hit the nail on the head and I want you to leave this area and get back to your camp pronto. I'll take the names and units of you three blockheads now, as you seemed to be enjoying it the most. You ain't heard the last of this, OK!" adds Lyndon.

The "white supremacists" walk away unwillingly, muttering under their breath about the nigger-loving officers. Frank and Lyndon then turn to the black soldiers and tell them to try and enjoy the rest of the evening.

As these disgraceful characters slouch off, Frank and Lyndon think of the very poor conditions suffered by the black airmen. With the air war becoming more and more intense they are becoming unfairly called upon to haul ammunition through mud, rain and fog. They are often even denied the right to sleep in decent beds and have to sleep in trucks. Instead of having normal food in the canteens with the other enlisted men, they were just given K rations. White officers weren't much help to them when fights broke out with whites; all too often they were commanded by inferior white officers who could be southern white supremacists. A very senior officer ordered an investigation into these serious concerns when it was found that the blacks were responsible for only ten per cent of the trouble with white soldiers.

18

THANKSGIVING DAY TALK

As Christmas is approaching, the Americans decide to improve their standing with the locals by throwing a children's party. Christmas Eve fell on a Friday, so that was the time decided upon to use the village hall. Warrant Officer Brian Armstrong from Chicago, a bull-necked, red-headed career soldier who had been at Pearl Harbor was nominated as Father Christmas by the CO—hard to imagine thought many of the ground crew enlisted men who had at times felt his wrath over minor breaches of discipline. The boys' mothers had carefully combed their sons' hair and found reasonably smart clothes considering the necessity for clothing coupons. The girls had naturally risen to the occasion and were a sight to see with their pretty dresses, carefully made by mothers, aunts and grandmothers.

They can't believe the food they are given as they enter the hall decorated with balloons, coloured streamers, United States and British flags with a model of a Flying Fortress on the stage. They are welcomed by the station adjutant, a major from Oregon, and invited to tuck in. Needing no second bidding, this they do readily and soon the sandwiches, cakes, jellies and ice creams are demolished. Now is the time for games which are organised by the Staff-Sergeant from Illinois, Brent Barker, a local radio announcer in civilian life. The airmen present not on duty that day join in enthusiastically in giving the children a day they won't forget. As they leave Father Christmas gives them all presents of fruit, chocolates and candy. It has been a wonderful day for public relations.

Frank has earned himself a reputation for being able to mix with the local children in a very relaxed and friendly manner and make them feel at ease with him, and their elder sisters at times. Earlier in the year he was asked to take a friend with him to the junior school in Diss. It was Thursday, November the 25th, Thanksgiving Day in the States. As always it was on the fourth Thursday in the month. He took Lyndon with him and arrived at the school at 11 am to be met by the head teacher, Mr. Hill. The children had been taken into the Assembly Hall, with neither staff nor pupils knowing why. There was considerable curiosity at this interruption to the usual school day. Had there been an enemy landing on the south coast? Was a heavy air raid expected? Was there to be some important visitor coming to visit the school? It was strange that even the teachers didn't seem to know.

Suddenly out of his office just behind the stage Mr. Hill appeared. There was immediate silence as he began to address the engrossed school. He told them that they were privileged to welcome two very important young men to talk to them; he knew how much they would be appreciated. At a signal to his secretary his door was opened and on stage came the two American officers who were introduced by the Head.

There was a gasp as these two extremely handsome young men came to the front of the stage. Their uniforms were so smart, beautifully pressed, made from quality material, campaign medals neatly arranged on the blouse, brown shoes highly polished, thus giving the overall effect of dashing warriors. The girls thought they were so handsome, the boys saw them as heroes to look up to.

Everybody thought that they were going to talk about the war and their experiences. Frank, opening the proceedings, told them that he and his buddy, an expression which amused the staff and children, were going to talk about an American custom which would be being celebrated on that very day. He and "Lootenant" Rogers thought that they would be interested in this event in American life which had no parallel in British customs. It was called Thanksgiving Day.

Frank trying hard to speak in a way not too difficult for them to understand tells them about one of the possible origins of this tradition. The British settlers had come together with a tribe of local Indians in the north-eastern part of America to celebrate the fine harvest of that year. The children were puzzled as they did not understand the term "British settlers" which was pointed out by Mr. Hill. Frank was used to every school child back home knowing about this. He tried to give a very brief history lesson, telling the pupils that his country's history was nowhere as old as Britain's. He is now becoming rather bogged down in historical detail, so asks Lyndon to rescue him.

"Sorry, boys and girls, but my friend is much cleverer than I am and he loves to talk about our history. As for me, it was never my favourite subject, except for stories about cowboys and Indians when I used to imagine I was Billy the Kid. Now I'm sure you would all like to hear about how we celebrate this great day — especially what we eat."

This causes broad smiles from the children who had been deprived of so much they had only heard about until the arrival of the Americans.

"Our main dish is delicious baked turkey after we have had some pineapple cheese salad. With the turkey we have all kinds of vegetables and cranberry sauce. I see you are puzzled by what this is. I tell you it is delicious and we may just have a surprise for you later. Now, if "Lootenant" Eberhardt would like to take over, he can tell you some more about what we have on this special day."

"Thanks, Lyndon. We usually have with the turkey several types of vegetable, sweet corn, mashed potatoes, different kinds of pies and my favourite here is pumpkin pie. It is a national holiday and really just a good excuse for having a wonderful meal and family reunion. Most people go to a lot of trouble to decorate the house with wreaths, fresh and cut flowers and all kinds of extras, often made by the children at school. Anybody want to ask any questions at this point?"

Hands are up everywhere with the majority of children wanting to know exactly such things as what is meant by sweet corn, pumpkin pie and cranberry sauce. At this point Lyndon brings out a bag he has been concealing under the table and shows these and other foods enjoyed on this big day. The children are naturally amazed and are made to feel more and more in awe of America. Not only do they have such incredible planes, such smart uniforms, such interesting accents, but also this wonderfully exciting, unfamiliar food. What a great country it must be to live in. All that most of them know is that it is a long, long way from Diss.

Many of them are interested in American films and want to know if they are friends with any Hollywood "stars."

"Not exactly friends, but I'm sure that you will have heard of Clark Gable. I see a lot of you are nodding your heads. Well, he came over to a base near here earlier this year. No, young lady, I'm not allowed to tell you which one or the whole place would be brought to a standstill if too many people like you got to know." At this, 11 year-old Katie Dowling blushed bright red.

It brings much amusement when one bright boy asks if they know Al Capone.

"I've never had that pleasure, son, and it wouldn't bother me if I didn't. I sure don't intend looking him up", was Frank's response.

"Sir, have you ever seen any cowboys or Indians?"

"I think that my friend here is the one to answer this as he is from Nebraska, real cowboy country."

"That's an interesting question, young man. Yes, I have certainly seen many of both, but it is not now quite like the western films which you have seen. The cowboys are just that and look after the cattle. The Indians are not warlike and more or less keep to their reservations. It is not quite as exciting as you probably imagine," answered Lyndon.

At this stage Mr. Hall said it was time to bring the meeting to an end as the young men would be tired. He thanked them profusely, but was reminded that there was one thing left to do. He was sorry that he had forgotten, but told them to form an orderly queue as they filed out. He called upon his pupils to show their appreciation of their guests which they did by giving Three Cheers. Frank and Lyndon said how much they had enjoyed their day in meeting such interesting and interested boys and girls.

In the foyer were two American Red Cross girls who gave the boys and girls bananas, oranges or candy as they went past. On the table were examples of Thanksgiving Day food.

On their way back to camp they agreed how valuable they felt the day had been and learned as much themselves as they hoped the children had.

19

FURTHER DISASTER AT FRANKFURT

It is late December 1943 and Frank's unit are summoned early one morning by the orderlies to attend a briefing. What can it be now? They seem to be continually on the go this month. The Forts and Liberators have heavily bombed every major German city and the men wonder what else is left. As Lieutenant Evans from Idaho says, they have had a wonderful tour of the country whilst being paid for by Uncle Sam. Not too many of them laugh as some of the men are coming close to the magical number of twenty-five missions. The most dreaded target was the capital, Berlin. Although they tried not to show it too much, that was the one they all feared. As it was the capital of the Reich, it was very strongly defended and, moreover, at a great distance. Although there had been enormous devastation to the German cities, there had been great losses to the RAF and the USAAF with hundreds of airmen killed, wounded or prisoners-of-war, if they were fortunate enough to escape their stricken planes, that is.

As you would expect, there were extensive flak batteries round the city. The fighters had not been such a problem since the arrival of the P-51 with its ability to escort the bombers there and back; the flak, however, was more fearsome as you could not fight back at it.

They go to the Ops. Room for the usual briefing on formations, weather systems, purpose of raid, defences and the points of integration with other squadrons. When the curtain is drawn back the string stretches from Norfolk to Frankfurt-am Main. The purpose for the raid is the destruction of one of Germany's most important communication systems. The men are told that they are to concentrate on the railway yards and do as little damage as possible to the civilian areas of the city. They knew all this, but it was impossible not to hit these areas. The RAF had been "carpet bombing" for some time, admittedly by night, but the USAAF bombardiers could not guarantee the kind of accuracy required so as to leave civilian dwellings intact, even with the famed Norden bombsight.

"Thank God it's not the Führer's backyard," says one of the bombardiers as they are leaving the Ops. Room.

"Perhaps not," agrees Frank," but it's certainly no tea-party. Frankfurt is a pretty tough place to go for an afternoon outing."

An hour later after breakfast which some enjoy and others don't, they climb into the trucks to take them to their aircraft on the hardstanding. Frank's is one of the furthest and there are many quips and jokes on the way there to try to lighten the atmosphere. They climb aboard with Frank, as is his wont, pulling himself up through the hatch at the front of the plane. This was the fourth Fort he had had at Thorpe Abbotts. It had been called "Hedy Lamarr" after one of Hollywood's most glamorous stars with a suitable painting of her towards the front of the fuselage. The skill of some of these artists was quite remarkable with such a range of names; it could be a Hollywood star (always female), the name of a town or state, the name of a wife, girl-friend or mother or some witty, ironic phrase. The name was often decided upon by the skipper whose wish was usually granted.

There are fatalities even before the planes have left the ground as one which was heavily laden with bombs was unable to gain height to take off and failed to clear the trees exploding into hundreds of pieces with all the crew killed. What a start to the day! Unfortunately, it was not uncommon for the Forts to have difficulty in taking off, even though the ground crews had given them such a rigorous inspection beforehand.

Without these dedicated ground crews there would have been no raids over the Continent. They were the unsung heroes who laboured all through the night preparing the planes. In winter they would work in freezing conditions checking the engines, loading the bombs and ammunition, checking bomb sights and gun turrets, repairing flak holes before finally starting to run the engines to check their airworthiness. They take an enormous amount of pride in what they do and treat their planes almost like huge family pets and their crews like members of the family, although it is wise not to become too close to them as some may not return.

Once in the air, it is necessary to be alert for other bombers coming into your airspace. This happens with "Hedy Lamarr," as to their horror they see a Fort heading towards them. The interloper, seemingly unaware of their presence, carries on into its collision course. Frank's pilot, Captain Ken Cragg, has no option but to go into a steep dive, a very dangerous manoeuvre given the bomb load. There is now the possibility of hitting another bomber on a lower level, a possibility even more frightening than facing flak or bogeys. With superb skill Ken Cragg manages to get the plane onto an even keel and straighten up just avoiding hitting a church steeple. All the crew are badly shaken, but it is agreed to carry on, even though they are now several minutes late in the timing for meeting at the rendezvous point. After making contact with the flight leader following frantic radio calls, they join one of the rear groups at a lower level than was previously planned. This is going to make further tests on Frank's navigational skills.

There are over 850 bombers heading for Frankfurt, but the weather is worsening and in mid-morning there is a signal from base to return. By this time, however, the leading planes are already over the Reich and to lessen the load for the return trip they decide to drop their heavy "cargo" as soon as possible, indiscriminately. Just before the Belgian frontier they see a large factory complex which they destroy. Frank's group at the lower level were uncertain of their whereabouts, particularly regarding the position of flak batteries and airfields. They are very low at about 11,000 feet near the Belgian coast when they are hit by the German gunners situated near an airfield.

Extensive damage is caused to the rudder, rear turret, starboard wing and fuselage. Two members of the crew are badly injured, including Frank with what appears to be a broken arm and chest injuries. It seems doubtful that they will be able to cross the North Sea, let alone return to base. Ken has already proved himself to be an exceptional pilot, but even his skills may not be enough. He alters course to try to reach an RAF fighter airfield in the south-east, Kent or Sussex, or even just a flat field.

The crew jettison as much as they can: guns, ammunition, oxygen equipment, are all thrown out of the plane to lighten the load as they rapidly descend. Should they bale out over the sea whilst at the minimum height possible or attempt to land? Given that it is December, the skipper decides against parachuting into the icy waters and carries on.

The white cliffs of Dover are now in sight and soon they are over Kent. They fly over an airfield which is too small for a B-17 and at the last gasp come to an RAF fighter airfield near what they later discover is Maidstone. They touch down reasonably comfortably, but then skid into a concrete gun emplacement. There is a mixture of bodies, parachutes and all kinds of equipment as the men try desperately to jump for safety. As they escape through the waist turrets at speed, they notice that the Fort has broken in two and there a serious danger of the gasoline exploding. Eventually they all escape with Frank having to be helped by the wireless operator, S/Sgt. Tex Cooper, an electrician from near Dallas. Amazingly, there is only one serious casualty as Ken Cragg's injuries mean that he will probably have to have his right leg amputated.

Following his troubles after the Stuttgart raid Frank finds it amazing that he is still alive to talk about his "adventures". Either somebody up there likes him, or he has used two of his nine lives.

After spending the night at the RAF base, the rest of the men are taken back to Thorpe Abbotts as Frank and Ken are admitted to hospital. Between mid-August and New Year's Eve 1943, The Bloody Hundredth have lost eighty planes, a number of losses hard to sustain. At least Frank is awarded the Purple Heart for his efforts which is some kind of consolation.

20

HISTORY MADE

Two days later Frank returns to his unit, leaving Ken behind. When he returns he discovers that he has been promoted to Captain in recognition of his leadership qualities and exceptional navigational skills. In addition he is awarded the DSO, Distinguished Service Order, for outstanding bravery and devotion to duty. His injuries will preclude his flying for some time, so he is offered the chance to become part of the Ops. team which he readily accepts; after all, did he not say after the Stuttgart experience that he would like to see what exactly went on in the planning division? This will allow him to see things from a very different perspective. He has often cursed them for some of their past decisions, but now he will perhaps understand their problems.

March 4, 1944, was a key date in the USAAF history as this was when they carried out the first daylight raid over Berlin. Frank had been involved in a fairly minor capacity in the planning of it giving his inside experience of missions over Europe. The planes took off under snowy conditions and as they flew towards their target the conditions quickly worsened. Most of the groups heard the order to return home, but one didn't. It continued to fly against one of the most heavily defended targets in Germany. Heavy squalls and thick clouds with alternate clear spells made the journey so difficult. Fighter resistance was swift, but they were saved by the arrival of Mustangs, otherwise they would have lost more than five bombers.

They had achieved little in terms of actual serious damage, but the greatest result was the fact that they did bomb the capital in daylight, a great propaganda victory which struck at the morale of the German hierarchy and citizens. Had not Goering himself said that you could call him a Dutchman if any allied plane dropped a single bomb on the Fatherland? The cynical Berliners were calling him just that after all the major cities and industrial sites had been attacked. Berlin itself had suffered a very severe mauling in late 1943 which became known as The Battle of Berlin.

Frank takes part in the planning of several raids over Germany at the beginning of the New Year as more and more notice is taken of his flying experience. His viewpoint has now changed as he understands some of the difficulties encountered in being able to plan missions with guaranteed success. He sees the planes take off after going through all the routine checks with which he is so familiar with the dedicated ground crews having played such a critical role. He feels for the men, imagines their feelings of trepidation mixed with excitement, their forced humour, with even the non-religious of them praying to be allowed a safe passage home. His stomach is churning in sympathy as he sees the Forts from his position in the control tower rev up the engines in turn, move into position, engines now nearly at full power, taxi onto the runway and with ever-increasing speed accelerate down it. It is an awesome sight to see these graceful miracles of engineering with their silver bodies climb into the sky. How can such an instrument of destruction excite so much admiration in its admirers? It is indeed a strange paradox.

Not that all the Fortresses have this idealised start to their trip to the Continent, as there continues to be too many instances of aborted take-offs when the plane has been too heavily laden to climb quickly enough or the pilot has misjudged his ascent and hit some building close to the airfield. The airfields are so close to human habitation, unlike in the States where they are remote. The effect so often is that the whole crew is killed or seriously injured—another ten men, good and true, sacrificed.

The men are now mostly on their way home; the nerve-racking part is receiving progress reports before awaiting their return. Just how many will return? How many empty beds will there be? How many letters will there be to write home to next-of-kin? Reports start to come through, usually optimistic, but often telling of heavy cloud over the target or of intense fighter and flak opposition. The raid over, with varying messages of success, partial success or disappointment, the bombers return, thankful for their escorting fighters as they battle their way back over enemy territory.

The counting is now about to begin as the first ones are sighted in the distance. It is about three in the afternoon as the leaders approach and all the buildings on the airfield are emptied with medics, ambulances, ground crews, all kinds of personnel emerging. Some pretend to be casual as they play around with a baseball throwing it to each other, but inside all are tense. The tiny specks are growing, the sun catching the silver fuselages. Not only the air force men are observers, but also the villagers who have now become so close to all these brave young men. Some of the planes are badly damaged with smoke pouring out of them, some have parts missing, such as engines, half a wing or most of the tail plane. One can see red flares being released from several of them as a signal that there are injuries on board.

Frank thinks back to an amazing story that came out in late 1943 as he sees so many planes limping home. There had been a raid to Bremen on a munitions factory which had been quite successful. However, on the way home one of the B-17s had been very badly damaged, having been attacked by at least a dozen fighters. One of the men had been killed, several injured and the pilot knocked out before recovering consciousness. Isolated from the rest of his group the pilot saw an ME 109 flying directly next to him, so close that he could see his eyes. The German pilot made gestures which 2nd Lt Brown did not understand. What he was doing was allowing the stricken, badly damaged plane to return to base as he could even see the bloodied crew members. At great risk to himself from his own side of being accused of treason, the German escorted the Fort to the North Sea before waggling his wings as a goodbye. When the crew told this story on return to their base in Suffolk, they found it difficult to make their colleagues and superiors believe this amazing story of chivalry, but eventually it was accepted.

Some of the sights which Frank sees are beyond belief as he could not understand how they had managed to return in such a condition. There were planes with all the plexi-glass at the front shattered, top turrets missing, undercarriages shot away, ailerons non-existent, many managing to make some kind of landing, but others exploding on touching down.

Many of the planes which had managed to leave German airspace badly damaged did not make it back to their base leaving a trail of destruction in East Anglia, Kent and Sussex with houses, farms, power lines destroyed. Some were lucky in that their pilot was able to land in a fairly flat field and even though the plane was a write-off, most of the crew could survive. The Eighth Air Force was paying a heavy price for its successes.

The number of missions now required for each member of the Eighth Air Force before being taken off action over enemy territory had risen from twenty-five to thirty. Frank is coming close to the magic twenty-five when this decision is made which he doesn't take to too kindly. His injuries are now healed and with the approach of D-Day more men are required for attacking key targets in France in preparation. Railroads and communication centres are to receive special attention. It is also thought that with the deterioration of the Luftwaffe the men are not in the same danger, therefore they can undertake more missions. The Germans have lost scores of fighters, but their greatest problem has been the loss of trained, skilled pilots killed, badly injured or prisoners-of-war. He is therefore sent back to resume flying duties with thanks for his efforts in the Ops. Room.

He stays at the station but this time with a different crew. Many of the men he was familiar with before have now been killed, injured, captured, repatriated back home or transferred to other units. As well as being known as the home of The Bloody Hundredth, Thorpe Abbotts is now also known as the Purple Heart centre of the Eighth, so many are their injuries.

There are not only the physical injuries, but so many of the crews have suffered dreadful nightmares from their experiences which have caused mental breakdowns. The USAAF is far more sympathetic to such people than the RAF. It is treated by the Americans as an illness, whereas in the RAF it is looked upon as a disgrace and they are certified as LMF, or Lacking Moral Fibre. They are stripped of their rank and forced to carry out such menial tasks as cleaning toilets.

There are stories circulating that many of the crews which have flown to targets in northern Germany such as Kiel, Berlin or Hamburg and have been badly hit have flown on to neutral Sweden where they will be kept as prisoners for the rest of the war. The reason may not be solely for fear of not being able to reach England, but it is a way to avoid the further terrors of having to notch up even more missions. This is strenuously denied by senior officers, but it is common gossip with crews.

The change around in personnel is so great that Frank's new crew is unknown to him and he is by far the senior member at twenty-five.

He makes immediate friends with Hank McCrae, a bombardier who also studied at the University of Pennsylvania, but in physics. He is 22, is a 2/Lt. and has been on several missions. He has an ironic sense of humour which appeals to Frank. He calls one of the majors on ops. Wyatt Earp as he likes to think that he is bringing in order and stability to his unit. A sergeant in the ground crew who tries to croon whilst working is soon christened Bing, but he sounds more like a wounded coyote. There is a young gunner in the crew with shiny white teeth and is forever smiling who becomes the Colgate Kid. This kind of humour, whilst simple, does help to make life that little more tolerable.

There has been some kind of a difference of opinion higher up the chain of command as "Bomber" Harris of the RAF wants to continue the policy of targeting cities in the belief that the widespread destruction of German industry, together with the killing of their workers and families, will bring the country to its knees. The joint Allied decision to attack the railroads and highways leading to the Channel coast he dismisses as a mere panacea.

The men have no say in all of this, but just have to do their duty.

Frank's unit attend a series of lectures concerning the importance of their job with the prime targets to aim for and the emphasis on railway marshalling yards and Luftwaffe bases. They still do not know where the actual sea-borne landings will take place and so a very wide area is covered to keep the Germans guessing. There is not the intensity of fighter opposition on these missions as they have been used to cover all over the Reich and in some ways there is not quite the same combination of excitement and fear. It is impossible not to kill and injure innocent French citizens; all those high moral aims at the beginning of the USAAF campaign over Europe have been proved to be impossible. Raids on enemy airfields can avoid a certain number of civilian casualties, but how can you do this when attacking factories and railroad targets? The view of Hank is that this legendary pickle barrel must cover an area the size of New York.

There had been a change in priorities for the role of the escorting fighters. Previously their task had been to stay close to the bombers in a defensive position, but the new commander, James Doolittle, argued that fighters were to be offensive weapons and should attack the Messerschmitts and FW-190s before they could reach the bombers. It had succeeded in a raid on Frankfurt when American fighters claimed between 120 and 200 enemy planes shot down, probable kills or heavily damaged, a number which required authentication.

Although the missions Frank was going on were generally less dangerous than before, he was growing very weary of being woken early in the morning and the ritual of breakfast followed by briefings for the day, weather reports, engine tests on the runway before taking off etc., etc. The new order by Doolittle to increase missions for each crew member from twenty-five to thirty continues to hit him hard as he was now in his twenties. He had not been too sympathetic previously when hearing of men suffering battle fatigue and being withdrawn from flying. It had been a case of not actually being able to see anything obvious, therefore it could be a ruse to be taken out of the danger. Now he realised that it was like an illness which was hard to deal with. After a raid on an airfield near Nantes he returned with a violent headache, dizziness and vomiting. He visited the medical officer who recommended that he taken off flying for a short spell and be given two weeks' furlough. He naturally went to London.

21

LONDON VISIT

London in 1944 was full of service personnel from all the allied nations. Many were stationed there permanently, but most of the Americans were there on a welcome leave, grateful to escape the tedium and danger of service life for a few days. There were uniforms of every description and the languages spoken made it seem like a modern day Tower of Babel. The whole atmosphere gave the impression of a holiday camp with people trying desperately to escape the wartime gloom. Inhibitions had been relaxed; you could sense that everywhere there was a search for food, friendship, liquor and sex.

A favourite spot for American servicemen was Rainbow Corner in the heart of the capital. It was run by American Red Cross girls and was made to be like an image of a drugstore back home with coke and hamburgers on sale for US currency. One could also buy fresh doughnuts with American-style coffee. There was a ballroom where it was possible to dance with volunteer hostesses and listen to the latest tunes and songs from the States.

Not surprisingly this is where Frank goes as soon as he hears of it. He quickly meets up with other airmen from bases all over Britain and from homes all over the States. He is disappointed that many of those from the Southern States are so prejudiced against black soldiers.

"Don't you guys realise that we are all in this together?" Some see his point, but others are so immersed in their prejudices that they are unwilling to give way. "I lost my grandfather and his family to those damn Yankees fighting for the blacks." It is hard to reason with people with such attitudes and to explain to them that there was more to the Civil War than just the abolition of slavery.

"Can't you fellas not understand that we are fighting now for the freedom of people to live their own lives in a democratic society where people are respected whatever their race, colour or religion? We are out to defeat the tyranny of a man who murders or imprisons people just because they are Jews."

Another airman, a S/Sgt wireless operator from Philadelphia, backs up Frank. "Do you not remember how Hitler snubbed Jesse Owens at the Olympics because he had won so many medals, defeating so many of his so-called master race athletes? Jesse brought glory to his, to your, country."

"I'd rather hear about Jesse James," says a bull-necked engine fitter from Missouri, "a real credit to his state."

At this point Frank has heard enough when he thinks of the atrocities committed by the James gang of criminals against Unionist soldiers. He doesn't know whether to hit this moron or walk away, which he wisely decides to do.

He walks around the Piccadilly area alone and is amazed at the number of women to be seen, mostly "professionals," but also ones looking for a good night out with an attractive American who would have plenty of money. The "career" girls are soon known as the "Piccadilly Commandos" or, less often, the "Hyde Park Rangers." With his good looks and smart uniform he has plenty of offers, and feels quite tempted with some of the classier ones. Perhaps surprisingly though, he still has Helga on his mind, and refuses the offers as he wonders what she is doing. He did think that he would remain faithful to her, but he is a young man and who knows what has happened to her. Should he succumb?

He carries on his tour of the area before coming to a noisy bar where there seems to be a very jolly atmosphere. There are forces from all the allied countries in there with a surprising mixture of ranks. He decides to join in. There is a rather attractive girl singing the latest songs from the shows on Broadway. She is wearing a figure-hugging electric blue dress, has auburn hair, a very trim figure and a lovely smile. After each song she receives rapturous applause and cries of encore. She almost looks as though she could double for Rita Hayworth; however, when she announces her next song, the illusion goes as she has a very strong London or cockney accent. Moreover, she has in close attendance two very tough-looking gentlemen, one with a broken nose and the other with various facial injuries. Neither smiles at all and it would be hard to imagine sharing a drink with them — they are obviously there for her protection from all these randy servicemen. Frank decides he has no further interest in her.

The atmosphere is not to his liking in any case, as there is a fog of cigarette smoke, the men are very untidily dressed, uniform jackets wide open, ties undone and language like the stevedores in New York. He knows that the men are off-duty and relaxing, but this is just not his scene. He senses that there could be fights any time as British soldiers and airmen are starting to bring up the fact that America was over two years late in joining the war. There is also the usual criticism of the Yanks' pay and food. He doesn't want to stay any longer in case fights break out, which he is sure they will, and he as an officer would be expected to intervene and issue disciplinary action. No, he has come here to rest, not carry on being an officer on duty. He decides to take his leave after drinking a pint of warmish beer.

He continues wandering round Soho in the blackout having to avoid bodies in compromising positions and continually being aware of the possibilities of having his wallet taken. He is still in a mood of depression, he can't quite get rid of his demons, so decides to turn in for the night.

Frank decides the next day that he would like to see some of this London which he has read so much about. Buckingham Palace, The Houses of Parliament, The Tower of London, Trafalgar Square are all on his "must see" list. It is a strange sight to see so many buildings fronted by layers of sandbags and windows protected against bomb blast by criss-cross layers of tape, together with the ever-present armed soldiers at the entrance. The people seem quite cheerful as they go about their business after the horrific bombing they have endured; one period earlier in the war they had endured fifty-seven consecutive nights of the blitz. The saying that "London can take it" epitomises their defiance. The Luftwaffe certainly does not seem to be breaking their morale.

Frank wonders what it is like in Germany in their cities which he and his allied colleagues have been destroying, particularly, of course, Bremen. He has felt at times very guilty of causing death to so many innocent people, but realising at first-hand what has happened to Londoners, he does not feel quite so responsible. What a miracle that St Paul's has remained almost intact when all around it is rubble. It almost makes him feel religious!

The following day a soldier takes him in a jeep to see the East End and the dockland area. Whole streets have been wiped out, ruins and debris everywhere. Where on earth do people live when their houses have been totally destroyed? Cockney wit has not disappeared as one elderly man tells him that they were thinking of moving anyway to a new house. A lady of about thirty holding hands with two young children wearing ragged clothing says with a sort of smile that it has done her Alf no harm with all the overtime he is having to do as a labourer. As they are talking, they hear the sound of an engine above. Everybody throws themselves to the ground as the engine cuts out. The rocket, as this is what it is, crashes two or three streets away with an enormous bang.

This is Hitler's latest weapon, the pilotless VI, or Doodlebug, which has just been brought into action. It is aimed indiscriminately in the general direction of London, so it is impossible to forecast where it is going to land. As the allied armies advance after D-Day their Channel launching sites are being overrun, forcing them to go further and further away from England. Bombing them becomes more and more a priority. Before very long a new rocket, named the V2, attacked London. This caused even greater terror as it flew so quickly it could not be seen, whereas at least the V1 could be shot down. This was a second Blitz on the capital in which nearly 25,000 people were killed or injured.

Frank's leave is now almost over, so he is due to return to Norfolk. Before going back, he feels he just has to see for himself the famous nightclub which boasted of never closing. There were up-and-coming comedians performing there and other acts, but the greatest attraction without doubt was seeing scantily-clad young women, even nudes, on the stage. To men who had been abroad lacking female company, this was indeed the highlight of their stay in London. He soon finds his way to The Windmill where he is able to come across a good seat. As a self-confessed student of female form, he has to admit that there are many very attractive ladies on the stage, but he soon feels that it is all a bit tawdry and cheap. The nude girls were not allowed to move as they performed what were known as tableaux vivants. In his somewhat depressive mood he soon tires of it all, particularly on listening to the inappropriate remarks by some of the audience.

22

EXPLORING THE COUNTRYSIDE

When he arrived back at camp his first duty was to see the medical officer. He explained to him what he had seen and done. From the way he spoke the MO did not feel that he was yet ready for further action and recommended a further leave from flying duties. The next stage was an interview with the CO, Lt. Col Martin James, newly arrived from the states. As a Lt. Colonel he is known as a Light Colonel, whereas a full Colonel is known as a Bird Colonel because of the badge of rank he wears with the symbol of the eagle. He knocks on the door, enters the CO's office and gives a smart salute before being told to take a seat. Lt. Col. James is quite tall, has closely-cropped dark hair and a scar on his chin. He is very brisk in his manner, but gives Frank a reassuring smile as he invites him to take a seat.

"I've been studying your record, Captain, and your experience as a member of a bomber crew is exemplary. You made a good impression on your short period in ops. Now where do you think your air force future lies? I see you came with a good report from college, so you obviously have something upstairs."

"Well, sir, I don't feel quite ready yet for returning to flying duty, but I don't want to be letting the guys down; they are suffering as I have done. I have seen them return from missions, just flop on the bed all gear still on. They wake in the morning, that is, if they have slept at all, report having very disturbing nightmares after what they have just experienced, talk in a disjointed way and have feelings of nausea."

"It's ok, Frank, within the privacy of this room you can call me Martin. I know what you are saying as I have been posted here from a spell in the Pacific bombing Jap outposts over there on the islands. You've had your Messerschmitts and Focke-Wulfs, we have had the Zero, no mean little plane with pilots who think it an honour to die for the Emperor-God. I'm afraid that this is what we are up against. We are doing our best to deal with the problem. However, I'd like you to consider being taken off flying duties and rejoining the ops. staff.

If it works out, I would recommend you to higher authority to be promoted to major."

"Thank you, sir, er Martin. That's very kind of you. How long do I have to think about it?"

"I'll give you two days and in the meantime have a further spot off duty, but stay in the camp area. Oh, and by the way, it has been noted what an impression you have made with the locals, especially the children. It means so much to forge a good relationship with the folks round here. The children may never forget us Yanks as they grow older, so you have done a fine job there too."

Frank salutes smartly again and leaves the room with all kinds of thoughts whirling in his head.

He had quite liked his spell as an operations officer when he had seen the other side of planning raids on the continent rather than being there in the action This new role, if he succeeded and were given a more active part to play, could be most interesting. But was he cut out for this job? Would he be able to take in all the information and make vital decisions firmly and confidently? He wasn't lacking in self-confidence socially, notably where women were concerned, but this was something different when men's lives were at stake. He also still had the feeling that he was letting the boys down and that he could be seen not exactly as a coward, but someone taking the easy way out. On the other hand, the possible promotion seemed very tempting and having been a major would look good in civilian life when he returned to employment.

He decided to ask his closest friends what their opinion was. Lyndon was the first one he turned to. He agreed that it was a difficult decision, given Frank's thoughts, but told him that he would be a fool not to take this opportunity.

"Look, Frank, you have done more than your share of flying, so I don't want to hear any more of this nonsense of letting your friends down. Nobody could possibly think that. As for you not having the brains to do the job, that is sheer bunkum. You went to a great university, so have no fears on that account. You have the social skills to be able to have a good relationship with senior officers. Knowing you, what should clinch it is this."

"I am eagerly awaiting this reason, Lyndon. Pray tell me."

"Frank, have you seen some of those dames who are air corps officers and you could be working with them? Gee, there is one at HQ who is the image of Greta Garbo, all cool and distant, yet alluring."

"No, can't say I have, but she's not really my type. Say you can find one like Merle Oberon and I could be interested. No, let's be serious, I still can't get my Bremen beauty out of my mind."

"She could have been killed or injured by our bombing, or she could be married. You just don't know. You've got to move on, Frank. You take this opportunity, it may not come again."

He decides not to discuss it with anyone else. He will speak to the CO and accept his offer. In the meantime he feels he would like to get some of that lovely Norfolk air in his lungs by taking some exercise. What better way of doing this than by going for a cycle ride in the surrounding countryside. He is still physically fit and is overcoming his deep worries, so a tour of the area is decided upon.

It is a beautiful late June day as he sets off alone. The villages are as beautiful as ever and so quintessentially English. The hedges, the fields, the picturesque cottages make him feel so much better. This is a real tonic after being in the claustrophobic confines of Fortresses with hardly anywhere to turn. There is freedom as he travels down the country lanes, listening to the birds and seeing the cattle and sheep in the fields peacefully grazing.

All is going well until he comes to a village where he has a puncture. Not knowing quite what to do he is wheeling his bike when he sees the back of a lady working in a beautiful garden with flowers of all colours. There is clematis and ivy climbing up the walls of the cottage which gives the impression of well-to-do owners. He stops and calls out to her. "Hi, madam, can you help me?" She turns round and he sees a lady probably in her mid-thirties. She is of medium height, rather attractive, dark-haired and slim and he notices she is wearing a wedding ring as she rests her hand on her spade.

"Yes, what can I do for you?" She recommends a garage at the far end of the village which could help him. "What brings a young American like you out here?" She says this in a rather playful, teasing way. "You are sweating rather a lot after your exertions. I was just about to call it a day and have a drink of some sort. You are welcome to join me, if you wish, that is if you are not too young to stay out of camp so long. Will you be missed?" All of this is said in a flirtatious manner, in a definitely upper-class accent which he finds impressive.

"I'd love to, ma'am, that's very kind of you, but would this be all right? I see you're married and perhaps the villagers would . . . . you know, gossip a little."

"Correction. I was married, but my husband was killed at Dunkirk four years ago when he had the bad luck to be left behind in the rearguard. He was an infantry captain. We'd only been married just over a year. Don't worry about the villagers, they are used to seeing Americans in the area and I don't give a hang about those with nothing better to do than have idle gossip. By the way, what is your name? I am Margaret, Margaret Atherton-Johnson."

After telling her his name, Frank then goes to the garage to take his bike for the puncture repair and promises to return. He leaves his bike there and on his return resumes his chat. He reminds her of his name whilst wondering why she has a double-barrelled surname. He expresses his sympathy over her loss. Of course she now wants to know more about him. He tells her about his life at home, his few months in Germany in 1939, his career in the USAAF, but doesn't tell her about his breakdown, or about Helga. He has enjoyed her company, but feels it is time he left.

"Yes, I understand military rules and regulations. I understand that our soldiers are told that when they arrive in Germany, they are not to be friendly, they call it fraternising I believe, with the local women. A fat chance there is of that being obeyed. Men have one-track minds. Do you think that you have been fraternising with me?" She says this with slightly raised eyebrows." I have enjoyed meeting you and you are very welcome to call again, if you are in this neck of the woods showing off your muscles. Now, your bike should be ready. Off you go, mustn't be late." She addresses him like a naughty schoolboy which he finds strangely quite sexy. He takes his leave and waves goodbye.

On his way home he thinks a good deal about this lady. He is very impressed with her as she has strong views, is attractive and has amused him with her provocative speech and manner. He has to admit that she is rather sexy; he has to go back. He has always liked to think that he was in charge of the situation where women were concerned, but she is definitely something different. Yes, he will find time to visit her again.

23

REVISITS NEW FRIEND

He returns to camp intrigued by Margaret. All kinds of thoughts are running through his mind. That dame sure has personality and yes, let's admit it, sex appeal. I think she rather fancied me. The whole day out has been marvellous and has done me a world of good. Lyndon was right, I still have feelings for Helga, but after five years, she may not even remember me and anything could have happened. I'm still a young man and anything could happen to me as well. What was it that our classics teacher used to say? Carpe diem, you only live once, or something on those lines.

He returns to base and two days later meets the CO with his decision. He is greeted warmly.

"Take a seat, Frank. Now, what have you got to say to my proposition? Have you thought about it carefully? I'm not putting pressure on you, but I think that you would be foolish not to take this opportunity." He said all this with a smile which made Frank feel at ease.

Frank says that he had thought it over carefully before deciding that he would take this offer.

"Attaboy, Frank, you are very wise. Now you will have to be posted to some place to the west of London called High Wycombe, code name Pinetree, where all the top brass hang out. It will take a few days to OK it all. In the meantime, make yourself useful and help out where you can until your official orders come through. From what I gather you will be missed here."

As he leaves, the colonel tells him he is sorry, but the promotion hasn't come through yet, it can only be a matter of time. He is disappointed, but thanks the CO for trying for him.

Frank gives a crisp salute to which the Colonel replies with a nonchalant wave of the right hand.

The next morning he decides that another bike ride would be in order and leaves at 10.am. There is of course no guarantee that she will be at home, but the exercise will be good for him in any case. He wonders if he will be able to remember the way through all these village lanes to the lovely home of the high-class lady. He eventually comes to her cottage seeing her yet again in the garden.

"Well, Margaret, fancy seeing you here again! I just got lost going for a little ride and I come across you once more."

"What a nice surprise! Amazing, isn't it that a navigator should get lost in such in such a small area as this? God help your crew when flying deep into Germany. I hope you don't take them to Berlin when they're supposed to be heading for Cologne and your colleagues are wondering what the fuck has happened to the rest of the guys. Good to see you, but now you're here, you can help me a bit. Take off that shirt and let's see that manly body as you grip the spade."

He is surprised at hearing such a well-educated lady using that kind of language, but in time he realises that this is not all that unusual.

"Are you making fun of me?"

"What on earth makes you think that, flyboy? But now you've done it, you don't look too bad. I could find you very useful," said with a twinkle in her eye and a suggestive smile.

Frank wonders if she acts like this to all young men. Perhaps she finds him especially attractive; he would like to think that he could be special. After an hour or so of toil, Margaret decides it could be time for a rest and so off they go into the house for a drink.

They have a gin and tonic which Margaret says she always has about this time in the morning. She then offers him another gin and tonic as she is having one, and then perhaps he would like a beer. He decides to take a chance and mix his drinks. He reasons:" What the hell does it matter? I'm off duty, even though it's only 11.15 and I have nothing till 4.30 when I promised to give a talk to some new fellas who have just joined us."

Margaret suggests that he would be more comfortable on the settee whilst she smartens herself up and prepares some lunch. Ten minutes later she returns in a flowery blouse, a little décolleté and a skirt about knee-length. He tries to stop staring at her without looking impolite, but finds it difficult to do so. She then goes to the kitchen to return two minutes later with some sandwiches and home—made cake. Frank asks her how she has made all this so quickly. She answers in that provocative way of hers. He continues to find his eyes wandering.

"Well, Frank, I just knew that you would be back very soon and a girl should always be prepared, don't you think? I could tell by the way you looked at me that you found me a little different, shall we say, and intrigued."

She apologises for the uninteresting sandwiches saying that with the present rationing system this is the best she can do. Frank tells her it is a miracle she has done as well as she has, but of far more interest to him is the sight of her legs with her skirt just over her knees. He doesn't quite know what to make of all this.

"Yes, you are right, you are very interesting. I've never met anybody quite like you, Margaret. You are very attractive, yet in a way a little forbidding because of the way you speak. You sound rather superior. What sort of background do you have?"

"I'm sorry you find me like that, I don't mean to be. It's just the way I was brought up. My father and mother were both privately educated as was I. My father was in law and mother used to write a bit. My late husband was from a banking family and that is my background. Father has died and mother lives in Sussex where I went to boarding school near Brighton. However, none of this stops me from being a normal person with likes, dislikes and feelings as with everyone else. Why don't you try to get to know me better?" This is said again with arched eyebrows and a half-smile.

Frank can feel that quickening of the pulse and the stiffening in his groin which the presence of this lady inspires with her appearance, gestures and speech. It is not long before all thoughts of the sandwiches, tea and cake have vanished. He puts his hand on her knee before they start to kiss, gently at first, then passionately. She takes the initiative by starting to undress him slowly with her hands lingering on and gently caressing each part of his body from top to toe, especially on his loins which drives him wild with desire. The gross excitement makes him desperate to undress her, but she is in charge and tells him not to be too impatient and he has to wait. As always, Margaret is in charge. She then allows him to take off her clothes, but he has to do it gently and not rush at it like an inexperienced lover. They are both now lying naked on the settee in an intimate embrace. He kisses her breasts with passion and sucks her erect nipples. What a wonderful figure she has! Before long they are making love with Margaret being on top in control as she tells him when she is ready to receive him. She insists they do it slowly to make it last and almost shouts out with joy as she and Frank climax together.

"Frank, you are a wonderful lover. Where did you learn that technique? I have not enjoyed making love like that for a long time. Do you do this with your other girlfriends, or shouldn't I ask?" "Margaret, you make it sound as though, well, I'm not quite sure, you are not exactly inexperienced in this field."

"Now, lover boy, you shouldn't ask a girl too many personal questions, now should you?"

Frank agrees, but still feels that he could be one in a long line to have enjoyed her favours. The time to talk to the new arrivals is now approaching, so he has to give his farewell. He promises to see her again and she tells him that he will be in trouble if he doesn't as he is such good company and an accomplished lover. On his way back to camp he thinks what a wonderful afternoon of recreation this been far from the battlefield. She is certainly so unlike any other woman he has known: sexy, seductive, experienced, intelligent and very classy. He has often wondered what it would be like to make love to an older woman; well, now he knows.

On his return to camp on his bicycle a jeep passes him with a handsome major from another squadron going in the direction of Margaret's house. That spark of jealousy which he has always had is rekindled as he wonders if the major is going to where he has just left. Surely, if that is the reason for the major's trip, she will not find him as welcome a visitor as Frank has been!

24

USAAF HQ HIGH WYCOMBE.

Frank has no time to return to see Margaret before he has to travel to High Wycombe and is only just in time to give a little pep talk to the newcomers before taking up his new position. They are full of interest in what he has to say, particularly about the German defences. How good are their fighter pilots? What about the flak? Is it easy to avoid? One of them thinks that you should be able to avoid most of the fighters with a skilful pilot in charge. Frank answers him with sarcasm. "Gee, why didn't we think of that before? Young man(said with the authority of a 25yr. old), when you are going in a bomb run and having to keep straight and level, you don't get much chance to do that. When you are flying to and from the target, they are like wasps round a honey pot and there is no time to do all this manoeuvring you are thinking of. Could I have the next question, please, preferably not one quite so naïve?"

The rest of the questions are rather more mature and sensible, but he feels rather sorry for the young man he spoke to rather sharply as the poor boy turns quite red with embarrassment. He apologises to him saying that he was quite out of order and he remembers when he was inexperienced. Frank feels that on the whole they are a lot of good kids who will learn.

On arrival at High Wycombe after a rather uncomfortable train journey and he has been shown his room, he is told to report to a Major Karl Bernstein in an office next to the principal planning room. The major is a small man with curly dark hair, in his late thirties Frank imagines. He is wearing a DFC ribbon on his uniform and has a rather brusque manner. There is to be no familiarity at this stage with Frank being addressed as Captain Eberhardt and his superior is "Sir."

The major goes over Frank's service record, stopping quite often to verify certain facts. He notes that the captain has been on some extremely tough trips and has gained respect for his skills as a navigator and for his excellent ability to work as part of a team. Having graduated from Pennsylvania State University is definitely to his credit. The only surprising facts he finds is that with such a record Frank has only one medal to show apart from his Purple Heart. He promises to make enquiries as to if one could be awarded retrospectively for what he has done. Besides, it would do his standing no harm in this new job. "The guys who go up there sacrificing their lives like to think that we on the ground know what we are talking about when we send them there. It would look good to have a DSO and bar to your name."

He is impressed with the accommodation he is given; silverware is placed on white napkins; freshly-cut flowers are in vases; mess waiters are dressed in smart white jackets—all so different from the rather basic quarters back in Norfolk. There are private rooms for all officers from mere lieutenants upwards. This is a building that was once an expensive school for upper-class girls and has been taken over for the war by the American military. It is a source of great amusement that at the side of each of the beds is a bell telling you "If in need, ring for a mistress." If only, the men think as their erotic dreams take over.

The Headquarters at High Wycombe is only four miles from RAF Bomber Command which allows close co-operation between the two and the ability to share facilities. Radar, weather and intelligence services are in close contact with each other and the results of the RAF photo-reconnaissance missions carried out mostly by Spitfires are also used by the USAAF. During Frank's time there the commanding officer is the charismatic General James Doolittle of the Tokyo bombing fame, when the Japanese capital was attacked from out at sea by carrier-borne bombers.

There is accommodation for over 12,000 personnel of both sexes, but what really staggers Frank is the construction of the site. All the important offices are built underground in three separate floors. Everything is covered with a deep layer of soil and at least ten feet of concrete. In several other ways the buildings had been made immune from bombing. There are emergency supplies of power, food and water, all of which makes Frank realise just how important is this nerve centre,

This was emphasised when he goes to his first briefing mission held by the General himself, attended by the entire staff of meteorologists, intelligence officers and navigation officers. Everything was gone into in meticulous detail by all the various experts. The priority target or targets for the following day's raids were decided upon, then the units to be employed and following this the fuel, the bomb loads and the amount of ammunition required, the airfields to be used, the timings of the departures and returns, the known flak batteries in the area, the airfields for the German fighters to use, and the rendezvous points for the formation of the groups. The main factor was the weather, of course, as poor weather would mean calling off the missions. The chief meteorologist was therefore absolutely crucial.

Doolittle is a no-nonsense man who expects concise details from the floor, but he would always listen to points made by even the most junior of the officers. Frank's contributions are welcomed because of his recent experiences of having actually taken part in so many important missions. At first he feels rather over-awed speaking up in the company of so many senior officers, but his confidence grows as they listen and sometimes act upon the points he was making.

He comes to realise just important are the staff at High Wycombe as everything the Eighth Air Force does is the result of orders from there. After listening to all the advice given, Doolittle and the senior officers would decide what the target should be. The orders are then transmitted to the relevant area headquarters to be then sent in turn to the individual stations. This is a daily ritual which makes Frank feel that he is at the nerve centre of the war in the air. He is now designated as an Air Intelligence Officer.

Frank starts to work the following day when he is given the task of helping to plan raids to Merseburg, near Leipzig in the east of Germany. This was an extremely important target as it was where synthetic oil was produced and also the home of several oil refineries. It was an extremely difficult target to bomb with accuracy as it was so heavily defended by flak and had even more guns to protect it than any other city in Germany. Much of this picturesque city would be almost totally destroyed. In addition, there was a continual haze or industrial fog near the target and the Germans had constructed several clever decoy installations. The bomber crews looked upon it as the most difficult target in The Third Reich. There are poor results initially, but eventually the relentless attacks begin to bear fruit. Frank is part of the team working on new tactics to bring these plants to a halt. His unit, after discussing several possibilities, suggests the use of saturation or carpet bombing with high explosives. This eventually causes one plant after another to be put out of action. The German war effort is greatly handicapped by this lack of oil and this will become a major factor in their defeat, especially when the Russians capture the Ploesti oilfields in Romania.

The Eighth continue to attack rail and road communications ahead of the advancing armies going through Europe, but in December there comes an unexpected major battle which they have to contend with. Hitler has made a surprising attack through the Ardennes which has caught the Americans totally by surprise at their weakest point, defended mainly by inexperienced, recent arrivals or soldiers expecting a little respite who are resting after their recent efforts. The American front line is totally overrun. The Panzers have come through difficult terrain to try to force a way through to Antwerp in Belgium, a major Allied supply port. They also hope to split the British and Canadians in the north from the Americans in the south and capture gasoline dumps. They have an acute shortage of fuel, so consider it absolutely vital to overrun these depots.

They are successful initially as in addition to the American weaknesses, the weather is so poor with heavy fog and icy conditions that the allied air forces are grounded. A great problem for the defenders has been enemy soldiers parachuting behind the lines dressed in the uniform of American MPs. They are men who have lived in the States pre-war, speak with a suitable accent, and are up with such details as the latest results of sports teams and recent films. They have been directing troops in the wrong direction and passing on false orders. When caught, they have been shot by firing squads. It is the job of Frank's unit to help prepare the response when conditions are suitable.

This happens just before Christmas when the fog clears and the Eighth orders every possible heavy bomber to attack airfields and rail centres the other side of the Rhine. Fighter bombers and fighters attack the retreating enemy forces now in full flight to be followed by the heavy bombers The armada of planes stretches back to England for three hundred miles, involving over twenty-thousand aircrew. The people of Norfolk, Suffolk and Cambridgeshire will never be able to forget this awesome sight for the rest of their lives. The white contrails from the planes when they reach a certain height framed against the deep blue of the clear winter sky are a thing of beauty. How can such a sight of almost poetic splendour be the prelude to the devastation and loss of human life to come? On this day the Eighth Air Force dropped more bombs than on any other single day in the war.

This initial attack is followed by further missions to overwhelm all communication centres within range. Bridges, railways, road junctions, main highways are all destroyed to prevent the movement of German forces and supplies. The Luftwaffe loses almost two hundred and fifty fighters in less than a week.

The Battle of the Bulge, as it became known, was America's bloodiest of the war and cost over nineteen thousand troops killed, but it cost the Germans about one hundred thousand casualties. The Eighth is then ordered to attack the centre of Berlin which would be a violation of the American stated principle that only targets of strictly military importance were to be targeted. At the beginning of February over fourteen hundred fighters and bombers are sent to Berlin, the largest force so far sent to a single city. They target German government buildings and railway stations which unfortunately are bound to be filled with refugees.

A few days later a heavy force of RAF and American bombers is sent to destroy Dresden, a historic town in the east of Germany. In the years to come this will cause extreme controversy with the airmen involved suffering great criticism. Although Frank's humane instincts did feel affected by these raids, as an ex-airman he felt far more sympathy for the men carrying out these attacks as they had no option when ordered to fly. He knows only too well what they have suffered.

Frank as part of this team feels very proud to be a member and to have contributed to its planning. He no longer has that feeling of guilt he had suffered on pulling out of the flying. Here there is no physical danger, but there is that sense of worrying about whether you have got your plans right with all those lives at stake. He is concerned too about the innocent French and German citizens who are being killed in this all-out war started by a madman. He often has discussions with fellow officers of the same status on the morality of it all, obviously out of the hearing of his superiors. Many of them agree with him to a certain degree, but many more say that "they" started it all, therefore, "they must reap the whirlwind." One of his section, a captain from Wyoming, is very angry with him and calls him a closet Nazi.

"When one sees all those newsreels of the Nuremburg rallies, one doesn't see too many innocents there."

"You should be back stateside as a conshie or washing down hospital wards!"

With this insult there is almost a fist-fight, but good sense prevails and they are separated and calmed down. Frank wonders if his feelings are genuine ones of compassion, or have they been brought on by Helga, and his generally good relationships with the Germans he had met five years ago, to say nothing of his ancestral background.

As the days go by, he is given more and more responsibility. To give him a fillip news comes through that he has been awarded a bar to his DSO for "Conspicuous Gallantry and Leadership Qualities." Major Bernstein has done what he had promised by recommending him for a retroactive award. The social life at his new station is not too exhilarating as they are all so busy at this nerve centre of the Eighth. At times they could be working a sixteen-hour day. He is getting on very well with his colleagues and there is plenty of banter about the superiority of their home states over others. Baseball and football news is devoured, again with much rivalry concerning favoured teams.

Frank is writing fairly regularly to his parents, but not as much as his mother would like. There is not too much that he can say beyond the routine as he is obviously not going to tell them about his present work. He is able to go to London once or twice with friends from his work and writes about the bomb damage there telling them how lucky they are to be so far away from the firing line. The city is swarming as ever with the military of all nations, so much so that it is difficult at times to hear a native voice. He goes into one or two bars, especially in the Soho area for there seems to be more life here, but still cannot get used to the English beer. Naturally, he and his friends are propositioned several times as Americans with their extra cash are looked upon as easy pickings and a few succumb. In spite of his other relationships with women, he still cannot get Helga out of his mind. He tries to, but she has made an indelible mark on him. His jealousy shows itself when he thinks that if she were killed in the bombing, then at least no other man can have her, but he then banishes this as such an unworthy thought and is ashamed of himself. His other women he has to admit have been the objects of lust, but with the beautiful German girl it was so different.

It is good for all of his colleagues to escape the continual planning of destruction so many miles away. The CO has told them that in carrying out this work they have to be as impersonal as possible by ridding their thoughts of all the casualties that will inevitably happen. Easier said than done as Frank's mind goes back to seeing his colleagues at various times shot down, and if lucky enough to bale out, parachutes not opening; on returning to base they have been badly burned or so seriously injured that this will have an effect on their lives in the future when they return home; worst of all, of course, are those whose bodies have been shattered beyond recognition.

The bomber war is becoming more intense as Germany's infra-structure is more or less gradually ground to a halt as the attacks continue on their installations and all forms of transport deep into the country. Berlin in particular is singled out for special treatment. In city after city the repair system breaks down with replacement parts becoming more and more difficult to obtain. The capital is attacked day after day by the Eighth Air Force and night after night by the RAF when vast numbers of bombers, escorted by fighters are dispatched to destroy the Luftwaffe. Another main target continues to be the synthetic oil plants, destruction of which grinds military transport so much to a halt.

One unusual job Frank is given is to help plan "Operation Chowhound." This is to drop food supplies to the starving people of western Holland. Because of the work of the Dutch underground in aiding the Allies in their attempts to take important bridges in Holland, the Germans had flooded large parts of the country and had begun to stop supplies of food reaching towns. The severe winter 1944-45

193

had caused the canals to be frozen, so hindering further supplies reaching the beleaguered citizens. After an appeal to the Germans they agreed for food to be sent, but only at allocated dropping zones. The planes flew in at less than five hundred feet with the enemy allowing them access. The British had a similar plan which was called "Operation Manna." As this is in the final few days of the war when Germany has all but capitulated, it is probable that the Germans are acting very sensibly in allowing this scheme to go ahead as those guilty of trying to obstruct the feeding of the suffering population could expect serious retribution for their actions. Frank was extremely happy that he has been able to help plan the details for this humanitarian effort to save even more Dutch people from dying of starvation.

25

LIFE IN GERMANY 1943-45

The situation in Germany is becoming worse, but nobody is ably to say publicly what they feel. Saying anything at all defeatist in the wrong place can lead at the very least to lengthy imprisonment and possibly torture or execution. The bombing has become a daily fact of life with Bremen receiving more than its fair share. It is amazing in these appalling times that the German civilian morale has not collapsed as "Bomber" Harris of the RAF was convinced it would, basing his whole strategy on this certainty. There are many instances of Allied airmen who have baled out being attacked by angry German citizens. They have been beaten up or often murdered by angry mobs. The irony is that so many are saved by German soldiers and treated as prisoners-of-war, unless they get into the hands of the Gestapo or SS first.

There have been several disasters inflicted on the country. The news from Russia is more and more pessimistic, despite unsuccessful attempts to hide the truth from the public. How can it be glossed over when the trains are still coming in from the east laden with dead and injured bodies? Too many families have suffered for people to be taken in by Goebbels' lies and optimism. At least many Germans are impressed by his willingness to visit the bomb-devastated cities, whereas the Führer is never seen in such places as though he refuses to acknowledge that such things could happen.

The attack on the Ruhr dams, whilst perhaps not as effective as the Allies had hoped, has done so much to damage German morale. How could allied bombers penetrate so deep into Germany without being detected? The bomb plot against Hitler has aroused feelings of varying strength: fervent Nazis are outraged, demanding draconian revenge on the perpetrators, but many more, if truth be told, are silently disappointed at the failure. There are trials held under the jurisdiction of Roland Freisler who metes out death sentences to hundreds of people including the families of suspects. The Führer's hitherto favourite commander, Erwin Rommel, is one of the conspirators and is allowed to take his own life, rather than face a mock trial before being executed. Hitler hypocritically gives him a state funeral to try to cover up his treachery. Hitler sees his survival as proof of his God-given powers. When the German army attacks in the Ardennes, taking the Americans by complete surprise, their early success once more gives him ideas of supernatural powers. A further proof of his infallibility is the death of President Roosevelt in April 1945 which can only mean that he is meant to overcome all his enemies and lead the Reich to glory. The Nazi element is governing people's lives more than ever. It is not uncommon to see bodies hanging from trees or lamp posts for real or imaginary "action prejudicial to the state."

In reality "The Thousand Year Reich" is in its last throes.

Against this background, the Wassermann family try to live as normal a life as possible. They are not exactly starving, but food is scarce, even for Klaus. Helga's experience of the bombing of Bremen and Hamburg had led her in her anger to volunteer for duty with the Luftwaffe. They soon realise that she is a smart girl and place her in the operations room plotting enemy bombers and giving directions to the fighters to intercept. There are so many raids on her home city that she is kept extremely busy. Helga feels that she is making some contribution to her country's cause. She had little time for a social life except the odd visit to a bar with friends. There were the odd dates with young men, but nothing too serious. After all this time and all that had happened, she still thinks of the handsome American boy who had taken her maidenhood and had charmed her with his foreign accent, his good manners and obvious love for her. What had become of him? Perhaps he had been killed or seriously injured in the war. She has little doubt that he would have found some other young lady to charm when he had returned home, so better forget him — if possible.

The Allies now have complete mastery of the skies, so it is thought that she will be of more use to train as a nurse as the hospitals are being overwhelmed, not only with victims of the bombing and badly injured soldiers, but also with refugees from the east fleeing from the Russians. She is assigned for training to the hospital opposite the barracks in Delmenhorst.

Herr Wassermann has had a nerve-racking time in the docks which have been the targets so often for Allied air-raids. However, he is a man with an iron constitution and has just carried on, whilst realising that he has been lucky to avoid death or serious injury, even though he has had several near-misses. He is much admired by his colleagues for his courage and determination. Only his family know how much he has come to despise the regime.

Frau Margrit Wassermann, although sick with worry about her husband and son, has been a tower of strength to the family, making sure as much as she can that there is always a meal on the table. Every time Klaus returns home after his long day at the docks she greets him with a hug and a large mug of ersatz coffee. She is longing for the war to end and with it Adolf Hitler's capture.

Their son Karl, now 22, was soon drafted into the Panzers. He saw action in Russia before becoming part of the army which attacked the Ardennes. After its initial success he was one of several hundred taken prisoner by the Americans and the last that they heard of him was that he was a prisoner-of-war somewhere in England and in reasonable health. His family are so grateful that he has not been killed or badly injured. His thoughts on the glory of Nazism have been transformed now that he has seen its effects in action. His family believe that their son will be treated much better by the Allies than he would be by the Russians, so this is some consolation.

Bremen's importance is underlined as it continues to be heavily bombed with a particularly deadly attack in August 1944. Helga had gone into the city to help collect some medical supplies when the air-raid siren made its mournful cry. Soon the bombs came cascading down. There were many mothers and children who could not reach the bunkers quickly enough; they were running through the streets in despair as the phosphorus bombs set their clothes on fire. There are people trapped in one bunker unable to escape because of the incredible heat which is melting the tarmac. Helga is luckily just in time to squeeze into a shelter which is already packed. The noise of the exploding bombs is ear-shattering and terrifying. Eventually there comes the welcome sound of the all-clear siren and as the begrimed and shaking people emerge, the sight is horrendous: water mains have burst, causing flooding on the roads, trams are wrecked, the station is in ruins — everywhere is chaos and destruction. Could Bremen take any more of this?

An all-too-common sight is that of slave labourers from Eastern Europe clearing away the rubble with guards above menacing them with rifles. One can see rooms of furniture exposed to outside view, bathrooms no longer hidden, a child's toy rocking horse in plain view and what could be priceless pianos damaged beyond repair.

Adelheide airfield near Delmenhorst, once a home for the Focke-Wulf, has now become a centre for displaced people and often Helga is sent there. The sights there and at the hospital in Delmenhorst are harrowing as are the stories which those suffering have to tell. Helga would return home after duty, often lasting twelve hours or more, completely worn out, physically and emotionally, and she is finding it difficult to engage in conversation with her parents.

From a carefree, happy, young student she feels she has aged at least twenty years. However, she is so competent a nurse that she has been promoted to Oberschwester, or ward sister.

Bremen and Delmenhorst are awaiting with trepidation the arrival of the advancing British troops.

26

RETURN TO BREMEN

Whilst Frank is at HQ, a notice is circulated asking for volunteers who are fluent in speaking the language to go into the area where the British are on the verge of occupying. They are to liaise with their British counterparts in discussions with the German authorities in towns and cities about to be taken over. One such vacancy has occurred for Bremen and its surrounding area.

Frank obviously applies and with his knowledge of the area and of the language he is sent for to be interviewed. The interview, however, is no formality and the colonel in charge asks him some searching questions. He is especially interested in knowing what his attitude would be to the local town authorities and the German citizens as a whole.

"Sir, my priority would be to see that the people are treated fairly and humanely. Although they may have lost the war, we must get them on our side in the rebuilding of the country and wiping out of Nazism. We have to help in whatever way we can and not make them feel humiliated."

"So you wouldn't agree with our late President, Mr. Roosevelt, that Germany should be made into a desert with all its industrial machinery destroyed?"

"No, Sir, I think we have done enough of this already, if I may say so. The country has to be allowed to get back on its feet."

"Interesting thoughts, captain. Now have you any other thoughts on what would be your role?"

"Yes, sir, we have to try and identify those who are still fervent Nazis and need interrogating. See if we can persuade them to admit the error of their ways. One bad apple as the saying goes. We don't want any of these in positions of authority. A priority must be to find as soon as possible those citizens who are relatively untarnished and have the intelligence and the confidence of the people. Then we put them in place, but keep our eye on what is going on in a non-too obtrusive way. We must also see that we address the question of food supplies. Keeping them in near starvation is a sure recipe for further trouble."

"Quite a speech, if I may say so. I like what I have heard from you. Some of the guys who have been in here were all for shooting every kraut and did not have too much vision of the future of the country. Major, you seem to have the foresight we need for this particular difficult job. I see you started when I addressed you as major. We need you to carry some status as I'm sure your British oppo. will be that at least. The rank will only be temporary to begin with, but in any case, I haven't seen anything in your records to show your interest in a permanent commission."

"No, sir, I hope to return to my original job in the states."

"OK, that will be all for now, major. We'll send you full details as soon as possible when this little struggle is over, which will be very soon."

Frank salutes smartly and leaves the room with a thousand thoughts buzzing through his mind. How proud are his parents going to be as he, a reluctant warrior, achieves the rank of major in such a short time and is selected for this important post in Germany. Most of all, however, he is thinking of returning to Bremen and Delmenhorst to see what he can discover in the area so fond in his memories. He knows there will be great changes, but how great? There will be enormous architectural damage he knows, but what about the people? He had found most of them friendly enough once he had got to know them, but now he is a different person. The once naïve, friendly young student has become an officer with authority in a conquering occupation force. Will he now have to keep his distance and be rigidly formal? Would he be welcome if he went off duty into a German bar, if indeed there were any still standing? Would this be allowed in any case? How strict is this non-fraternisation rule which he understands will come into immediate effect, not just with girls, but also with every civilian? At the back of his mind, of course, is the one in a million chance of meeting Helga. Wishful thinking!

The war comes to an end with the unconditional surrender to Field-Marshal Montgomery on Luneburg Heath of all German forces in North-West Europe on May 4, followed three days later at Reims in France by all German forces also surrendering unconditionally to General Eisenhower. Frank is not too happy about the "unconditional" surrender as he feels that the country must be allowed to recover without this restraint.

Major Eberhardt is now awaiting further orders before proceeding to Bremen.

He arrives at Bremen after a sea crossing to Holland. The comparison of this with his last such journey cannot but recall all kinds of memories; he has advanced from a fairly immature student into an experienced air force officer with what seems like twenty years of memories in only just over six years. Maybe one day he could write a book about all this, but what to leave out could be the problem. He hasn't finished yet as he now has a new task, not as dangerous physically, but nonetheless a great challenge to his powers of diplomacy. He has proved himself as an airman and as a behind the scenes planner; now he has to show his skills in a different way. Will he see eye-to-eye with his British counterpart? How will the new German authorities who will be soon in place react to their conquerors, as that is what they are despite Frank's dislike of the expression? It will be necessary to find out what quality of men these will be before anything constructive can be done.

Although the major part of the zone is under British authority, there is a narrow corridor to the North Sea which includes Bremen itself and Bremerhaven which are under American control; Delmenhorst is in the British sector.

He meets his new boss, a Colonel Roberts from Arkansas, with whom he feels an instant lack of rapport. He is rather sarcastic, saying he is a little wary of smart flyboys as he thinks they have too much glamour attached to them and their role can be overplayed by the military publicists. Not a great start, especially when Frank thinks of all those marvellous past colleagues of his who have given their all in their missions over Germany and occupied Europe. When he has had time to get to know him, he realises why he has this rather negative and insulting attitude.

He had been a Lieutenant Colonel in an infantry regiment during the German Ardennes offensive. They were one of those units taken by surprise and overrun. Most of them were killed, injured or taken prisoner. However, he and another twenty or so managed to stay hidden in a barn. When the advance units of panzers had gone past they started to try to find their way back to their own lines through the thick snow and freezing conditions. The journey was through heavily wooded country which made it easier to hide as did the rapidly falling snow which quickly covered up their tracks. They had no food or drink which forced them to drink melted snow. Their progress was far from easy for the men had to hide several times as they heard Germans in the area, so close at times that they could actually hear them talking. A sergeant who understood a lot of German said that they were complaining about the weather and a sergeant major who was rather too strict for their liking.

Another one was telling his colleagues that they would never come across Americans here as they had all fled, been taken prisoner or killed.

Before reaching the American lines, they had several more near escapes, such as almost coming across a tank in a clearing where the crew were resting, joking and refreshing themselves. By now the Americans had split into two parties, many of them suffering from wounds which were needing attention. On eventually finding their mates after such a harrowing experience, insult was added to injury as Colonel Roberts and his group were challenged at gun point. Germans had already been caught in American uniforms behind the lines; no chances were being taken. They were allowed in eventually and were taken off for food and drink.

What really upset the colonel was that so much publicity was given to the efforts of the air force when the weather cleared that the dreadful ordeal of these men in the pitiless weather, lacking food, continually on the run was hardly touched upon by the American propaganda machine. Instead, all their efforts went into publicising the massive US air offensive which took place immediately the weather cleared.

Frank can understand his frustration; however, he decides to leave it at that and agrees that the infantry have had one hell of a time. The colonel's knowledge of German comes from his maternal grandparents being immigrants from Bavaria in the early years of the century. His mother was obviously German and so many of the conversations with her at home were in this language. He gives Frank an informal oral test with very satisfactory results. The time spent with those workers in Bremen did give him knowledge of the vocabulary, some of it not necessarily to be seen in any text book.

On his first day he takes a look round the city, particularly the parts he remembers from six years ago when everything was so different in all ways. He was very upset at the state of the city with its ruined buildings and bomb-sites, the citizens wandering round like zombies, many with probably nowhere to go, trams still heaps of twisted metal— would this ever be back to normal? Yes, possibly in about ten years from now. Had he really been partially responsible for some of this? From such a great height you don't always envisage the damage below which you are causing, you somehow can feel detached from all this. The spots where he had been with Helga were at times unrecognisable. How could this have happened!

Before officially starting duty he decides to spend a Saturday taking a look at Hamburg, a place of happy memories. He borrows a jeep for the journey after a little bargaining with the motor pool. When he arrives there he wishes he hadn't bothered as it is so depressing, if anything it is even worse than Bremen: there seems to be hardly any building left standing and the destruction after the horrendous firestorms of two years ago is all too plain to see. What is amazing is that the Hotel Atlantic Kempinski on the other side of the lake from the firestorms is virtually untouched. He goes to look to discover that it is now the Head Quarters of the British Army of Occupation for the British sector. He enters from a far different situation from when he last saw it six years previously. He is made very welcome and cannot help but think of that promise made all those years ago by Helga. He then returns to Bremen with this feeling of guilt.

Once on duty on the Monday one of his first tasks is to visit what is left of the Hamburg Law School to see if there are any records of Helga. Unfortunately, the records have been destroyed by fire. He determines that as soon as possible he will find a pretext to visit Delmenhorst to see if there is still any trace there of her and her house. After several days of talking to Germans of all backgrounds about their present situation and questioning them on their political beliefs, he does manage to get a jeep to drive him to Delmenhorst. Colonel Roberts with whom he is now on much better terms after their first fraught meeting, has readily agreed as this town is on their agenda. The suburbs of the city are very badly damaged but as he is driven nearer to his destination there is not so much evidence of the air attacks. He gets out of the car in the middle of the town and there is that unmistakable smell of the lino factory.

His next port of call is to see if Helga's street is still intact. He has difficulty after all these years of finding it by road as he had previously travelled by train. At last he arrives there and stops on the corner. Yes, there it is just as he remembers it. As he is looking, some residents of the area seeing his uniform either look the other way or give him a surly glance. These are the people the Allies have to win over. Should he knock on the door or drive off to another part of the town? As he remembers from his school days, the English teacher in some such situation would have said, "Discretion is the better part of valour." What would happen when the door was opened and one of Helga's family were to see an American officer standing there? Her parents probably would not recognise him; they would be shocked to see a member of the occupying forces standing there, not understanding why. Their son would probably be aggressive, whilst Helga herself . . . who knows? Better to think more about this.

He then decides to go to the hospital opposite the army barracks on the edge of the town. This was allegedly bursting with Displaced Persons from the east of the country as well as the usual sick and injured patients. Some of these DPs could be well worth having a chat with, not a formal interrogation as then you may find out more as they would be far more relaxed. There is always the possibility amongst other bits of useful information that there could be prominent Nazis on the run from the Russians in the east. Some of the refugees had come perhaps merely to join up with families in the west, but most of them preferred to be at the mercy of the Allies rather than the Red Army. There is more than a day's work here, so he contacts the colonel to ask for an extra day. This is granted.

He speaks to many of these people, most of whom seem to be perfectly normal and innocent, but those he has doubts about he refers for further questioning to the British MPs who are close by in the barracks opposite. He also meets there the British soldier who is acting as Town Mayor, Major Jack Wolfe. He tells him that the takeover of the town by units of the Black Watch, amongst others, had been quite smooth with little resistance. There have not been any signs of trouble from the townspeople; if anything, they were rather cowed and seemed pleased that it was all over.

The British authorities do have their eyes on certain people in the town who could have been members of the Nazi party, but they are carrying out further undercover enquiries.

Frank decides that next day he will have a further look at the hospital where there will be many ex-members of the armed forces. He will, with the help of a British colleague, have little "chats "with them.

27

RE-UNITED

The following day he is driven directly to the hospital. On his journey there the town's citizens move deferentially aside as the jeep with the American star makes its way to the hospital through the narrow streets. He and his British counterpart who has come separately, Major Keith Bennett of the Royal Artillery, are directed to the ward for limb injuries. The major was studying languages at Cambridge University where he was in his second year. He left to join the RA which was father's regiment. His German, although good, is not as idiomatic as Frank's as he has missed out on his year in Germany which is part of the course. They speak to two or three soldiers each from whom they learn about their battle experiences, that is those who wish to say something, but some of them are unwilling to talk. The talks do not reveal too much out of the ordinary, but it is interesting nevertheless. They have one ex-Panzer from Bavaria who gives the impression that he could still have Nazi sympathies. He is earmarked for further attention.

Their next assignment is to the surgical ward where people awaiting operations will be placed. Some of them are in a very poor condition being in no fit state to be spoken to. Others, however, are able to have a conversation, so Frank and Keith talk to these. Memories of the Ardennes and defending the borders of Germany in the Rhineland come flooding out with most of them expressing relief that it is all over.

When Keith is speaking to an ex-Luftwaffe airman, something attracts Frank's attention. Out of the corner of his eye he sees the back-view of a nurse bending over a patient to give him an injection. From this angle it could be Helga, so he goes over to find out. When he speaks to her, she turns round to reveal that it is not her. Frank apologises, saying she had reminded him of a certain Helga Wassermann he had known years ago. "Oh Helga, there is a sister called that in the burns unit. She does come from this town and I believe she is on duty there today. How on earth do you know a German girl?"

"Oh, it is a very long story. I'll tell you about it later."

After offering his thanks, Frank is now undecided as to what to do. His instinct is to go straight there; his uniform will ensure easy access. What though if it is another local Helga? What if it is her and she doesn't recognise him, or worse, doesn't want to know him? What a blow to his pride that would be. He just has to go or he would never forgive himself. What if the non-fraternisation rules were to prevent him from meeting her after he sees her? He hesitates then, before asking a nurse for assistance to find the burns unit.

It is the other side of the hospital and he sees many cases on trolleys being wheeled from ward to ward. He quite likes the smell of the hospital as he goes on his way. After his lengthy walk he finds the burns unit and looks through the window with a mixture of excitement and trepidation. He is asked by a doctor who addresses him as Herr Major if he can be of assistance. He answers that he is looking for someone he believes is in there but will find "him" himself. At first Frank just sees a couple of nurses who certainly aren't Helga. Then out of a side ward steps a rather attractive dark-haired girl. Can this be her amidst all these dreadful sights of horrific burned bodies? She has her back turned as she deals with a man who has a badly-scarred face. When she has finished, she half-turns and upon seeing him exclaims in a loud voice, "Oh, mein Gott! Is that really you?"

Those who are able turn their heads in disbelief; how can a German nurse know an American officer? They are both completely overwhelmed and don't know quite what to do. She says out of the hearing of the others that she will be finishing at 5 o'clock and asks if they could meet in one of the side rooms on the pretext of discussing one of the patients. The rest of the afternoon finds both of them in a daze, more so for Helga as at least the meeting wasn't such a complete surprise for Frank. Helga had shown total amazement, but was there any sign that she felt for him the way she had done on their painful parting all those years ago?

The time goes agonisingly slowly for both of them as 5.00 pm approaches. Frank feels guiltily that he is just going through the motions as he goes round speaking to patients. At one stage Keith asks him if he is all right. He says he just has a touch of hay fever which in reality he has never suffered from. He makes some notes before telling his colleague that he will be back at HQ later as he needs to speak urgently to one of the ward sisters about a patient's background. This gives him a perfect excuse for using one of the adjacent rooms.

The appointed time arrives. Frank is first in the room, not wanting to be late, just as happened on their first date in 1939. Now he has a closer look at Helga and sees that although she is still very attractive, she does look a little careworn. She probably has the same thoughts about him. They are both wordless as they look at each other, neither daring to break the silence. At last after what seems several minutes, but is in fact a mere twenty seconds, it is Helga who speaks asking him "Wie geht's?" Frank says that he is fine, but what about her? The ice is broken, but she in particular is rather guarded in the conversation. They both explain why they are there, what they have been doing, how life has been for them. From the conversation they realise with grim irony that she could have been plotting to shoot him down over Bremen.

They both needlessly apologise, but it is very easy to understand their feelings. Helga bursts into tears at the thought and as though a screen has been drawn away tells him she has always loved him, even though he was technically an enemy. She wonders how many girlfriends he may have had since he left her. Without going into too many details he tells her that they have only been "friends", nothing serious. In her turn she also says that any boyfriends have been just that, and she has always thought of him wondering what he has been doing back in the States. Frank cannot believe this and throws his arms around her and kisses her. The ice has now been broken; when can they meet again?

She responds passionately, but is worried as somebody could see them. "Das ist mir egal. I don't care now I have miraculously found you." The problem now is going to be the non-fraternisation laws ordered by The Supreme Commander. These laws forbid any friendliness with any German citizen, man, woman or child. General Eisenhower wanted them to be made fully aware of their crimes. There was even a directive that "In heart, body and spirit, every German is a Hitler." All this was against Frank's thinking as Germany could not drift into even more chaos. It would be impossible to make any progress with this kind of action. In any case, certainly as far as women were concerned, this would be more honoured in the breach than the observance. These GIs had been fighting to the death on the land, on the sea and in the air under appalling conditions with a lack of female companionship. After all, they were red-blooded young males far from home.

It would be impossible not to include the German population if their country were to recover. Had the lesson of Versailles not been learned when extreme conditions had been forced upon them? Look what had happened as a result of that. How could you allow a country of such size and potential to be made into a wilderness? All these thoughts were going through Frank's mind. The question now was how to make his way round these restrictions, especially as he was in an important position and a major in the USAAF.

They do manage to meet secretly with great difficulty before, as was inevitable, the rules become more and more relaxed. They had decided that they wanted to be together as they had never really forgotten each other throughout all the turmoil. One day on the banks of the Weser in a wooded area they make love again and decide that whatever the difficulties they would never be parted. It was soon to be Frank's date to be released from the military when he would be sent home to the US, so they have to think urgently about their future. It would be necessary to meet Helga's parents again, however difficult this could prove for all four of them.

The idea was for them to obtain a visa for Helga to travel to America as soon as possible. This could be difficult, but it would be easier if Frank's war record were to be taken into account and they were to be married over there as soon as this could be arranged. Helga could continue her law studies, if a suitably liberal college were to be found, one which would not harbour grievances against a former enemy.

Helga decides that it would be better if she were to warn her parents before taking him home; it would also be diplomatic if he were not to be in uniform, but dressed in civilian clothes. She chooses what seems a suitable time to talk to them when they are in a good mood. They talk about all kinds of things before she says," Mutti und Vati, I have something important to tell you." They make one or two flippant remarks before they realise that she is in earnest. At first hesitatingly, then rapidly, she tells them about meeting Frank in the hospital. One thing she does not tell them is about his war career and bombing Germany, Bremen especially. They are astounded, even more so, when she tells them that she wants to be married and live in the States. She is asked a thousand and one questions about this shock news. Eventually Herr Wassermann agrees that at 24 she is old enough to know her own mind and the war is over after all. His wife, realising how well the Americans appear to be fed, wonders if perhaps he could arrange for them to have some real coffee, nor would the odd tin of ham or peaches go amiss.

It is agreed that he comes to see her parents to ask for her hand in marriage," but please tell him not to come in uniform!" Frank comes but feels not a little uncomfortable. Is it not an ordeal at the best of time to ask a man for permission to marry his daughter? In these circumstances, however, it is even more difficult. The meeting begins very formally with a slightly cool atmosphere, but as they speak it becomes more cordial for the parents realise that the pair are genuinely in love. They have so many questions to ask the young people before being completely satisfied with this giant step in her and their life. They are concerned about what their relatives and friends may feel. Margrit had an aunt and family whose home near the main station was destroyed, many of her husband's colleagues were killed or badly injured and their homes destroyed in the dock area. What will their neighbours think if their daughter marries an "enemy" and goes off to his country? After all the bombing of the Bremen docks where Herr Wassermann was working, Frank dare not tell them of his part in this; he says instead that he had a desk job working on supplies. As the Wassermanns already have a son who is a prisoner in England and do not know when they will see him again, the thought of their daughter going overseas is so upsetting.

He puts them slightly at ease by saying that she has a great chance to resume her studies in his country when they are married. They agree that this would be good as her prospects for work or continuation as a student in Bremen are not good. He reassures them that he will make sure that she keeps in constant touch with them by letters. As soon as is possible, they will try to visit Delmenhorst. They feel that he will look after her and that this is what she wants to make her happy. She throws her arms around them with tears in her eyes and cannot thank them enough for being so understanding. Even her father, not used to showing his emotions so openly, is struggling to stop crying, whereas her mother is sobbing uncontrollably. Frank feels quite guilty looking on, but he much appreciates it when his future father-in-law embraces him after shaking hands. Her mother hugs him and kisses him on the cheek. He is then introduced to a custom he was unaware of. If it feels the time is right to change from the formal "Sie" to the friendlier, more informal "du" in greeting, Germans, with a drink in the hand, cross arms and taste what's in the glass; this little ceremony shows the new relationship. He really feels accepted when he is called Frank and he is invited to call Helga's parents by their first names. In such a formal society as Germany this is a real breakthrough.

When duties allow he comes to see Helga or perhaps meet her at Haus Helgoland which has miraculously remained intact amidst all the bombing. It is a mere shadow of itself as the locals do not have the money to spend and there is an atmosphere of defeatism and gloom. They only go there a couple of times as its magic has gone. Wandering round the streets is too heartbreaking for both of them as they see piles of rubble, some areas like a desert, and so many rootless children, many probably orphans, wandering around aimlessly.

The saving grace is that they are both kept busy in their daily jobs. There is no let-up in the hospital as more and more refugees are flooding into the town from the east. So many of them have no idea where the rest of their family is. The tragic stories are so moving, but the medical staff must try to keep as unemotional as possible. Frank is doing his best to cope with the mounting workload as he and Keith are called upon to settle disputes, help people to find some kind of accommodation and feed those urgently in need with the rapidly decreasing number of calories they are able to feed on.

So far they have only found two obviously genuine Nazis, two prison guards, one from Bergen-Belsen and the other from Sachsenhausen concentration camps. They have been recognised by former inmates as brutal guards who have been trying to hide as bona-fide refugees. One of them it turns out was especially cruel towards Latvian Jews, people from his own country. The other one from Pomerania, an exceptionally ugly person, seemed to take a delight in persecuting women. After close interrogation the accusations are seen to be genuine as they are sent off for further questioning to join those who had merely caused suspicion.

Frank was so disgusted with them that he became very close to losing his temper. Turning to the Latvian, he addressed him in strong terms: "Du bist eine Schande für dein Land und deine Leute!"

"Ich habe nur meine Pflicht erfüllt."

"Das Gericht wird das entscheiden!"

He told the Latvian that he was a disgrace to his country and to humanity. When he answered that he was only obeying orders, Frank said in an icy tone that that would be a matter for the court to decide.

When they are ordered to be led out they are accompanied by the jeers and hissing of those who had known them and have to be separated by the hospital staff from patients who wish to attack them.

28

RETURN TO USA

The time is now approaching for Frank to return home. His father has already told him that he has a job awaiting him at his old place. Everybody there is so eager and impatient to see him, all dying to hear of his experiences. They have heard so much of what he has done, but of course he has omitted so much when writing to his parents. He hasn't seen himself as a hero, but as a young man merely doing his job as a citizen of his country. What he has seen and done has made him feel more than three years older. He thinks about those wonderful guys who have paid the cost of their dedication to the cause with their lives or frightening injuries which have disabled them, or in some cases may have disfigured them.

His problem now is to gain the necessary visa and other paper work for Helga to go over to the States. The bureaucracy is truly formidable. Has she had any links with the Nazi party? Can she verify that she hasn't? Can she swear on oath that her wish to come to the USA to be married is genuine and not just a way of gaining exit from Germany? What about working in America? What are her qualifications for this? Will she be accepted by an American university? Her head is going round in circles. She is told that she will be notified by post as soon as a decision is made.

Meanwhile, Frank has said his farewells at Wycombe Abbey and so is ready to return home. He needs to know that Helga will be able to follow him; he hasn't even told his parents about this, as he wants it to be a surprise. The time comes when he has to leave as his period with the USAAF has come to a close and he has finished as a major with a couple of service ribbons, a DSO and Bar and a Purple Heart. He flies home in a service plane, but this time there is no feeling of responsibility or of danger. What a relief! He is greeted ecstatically by his family and friends to be invited to far more receptions than he can deal with as grateful as he is.

Back in Germany Helga eagerly awaits every post, but day after day goes by and still the authorities are not letting her know their decision. The postal service, not surprisingly, has yet to achieve its pre-war efficiency, but even so, an answer should have been received by now. She has not heard anything yet from her future husband, but this is not so surprising perhaps. She has to just carry on waiting and hoping. There is also the matter of having to give her two weeks' notice which just adds to the time. When exactly does she book her passage for the trans-Atlantic journey?

Frank has already started to work and is enjoying meeting old colleagues once more. Many are still employed there, some in more senior positions. The sad news is that two of them have been killed, one in the navy in the Pacific and the other on D-Day. His parents hadn't told him because they didn't want to upset him. If only they knew how often he had had to come to terms with death. He is very impatient at the lack of news from Germany and manages to send a telegraph to the Delmenhorst hospital asking for news of Oberschwester Wassermann.

At the end of July Helga receives news at last that she is free to go to join him. She books the first possible ship to go from Bremerhaven to New York. All is arranged, she could reach America by the middle of September. Filled with joy, she sends him the good news. He receives her letter and is so thrilled that his workmates wonder if he has just found out that he is the benefactor of a rich relative's will.

"What! Is this that Brünnhilde type you knew all those years ago? You're a dark horse. Why haven't you told us about this before?"

He promises to tell all to his friends over a drink after work one evening. It is noticeable that there is a spring in his step after this and they wonder if he has started training again for football. He still hasn't told his parents, however.

The time comes for Helga to board the ship after she has had to endure even more formalities. There are so many wanting to go to the Promised Land that the boat is almost overcrowded; the passengers listen more intently than ever to the lifeboat drill. Some are like her in that they are going to marry an American serviceman, but most are those who just want to escape the chaos in Europe. There are also those who have families from a previous generation of immigrants and so have somewhere to go when they arrive there. With so many fellow Germans on the boat, Helga is not short of conversation. Many of her new colleagues have horror stories to tell the other passengers about the Allied bombing, or the ruthless advance of the Allied armies through the country. They are overjoyed to have escaped the Russian invaders as stories are filtering through of their raping of German women. So many of the passengers have lost fathers, husbands or sons on military service that America represents a fresh start for them, a new life.

Finally the boat reaches New York with most of the travellers having experienced sea-sickness, as this is their first ocean-going voyage. Helga says goodbye to her new-friends to attend the immigration procedures. She has noticed Frank on the quayside and waves frantically to him. He has not been able to spot her with all those others surrounding her eager to leave the ship with its unappetising food and rather basic toilet facilities.

She is disappointed at not being able to make contact with him as there are so many more checks to undergo. She is asked more or less the same questions as at Bremerhaven and gives exactly the same answers. She is amazed at all the bureaucracy she has to deal with before finally being cleared and leaving the ship.

Still Frank cannot be found as he too has had to answer a series of questions to verify his story and pass through several obstacles: officialdom and finding the way through so many passengers and doorways with confusing entrances and exits. Has she in fact come on this boat or decided at the last minute that she could not face leaving her family behind to come to a strange country? Then he sees her struggling with her luggage, not being helped by any of the staff near her. What manners from his fellow countrymen! She sees him and waves excitedly and at last forces a way through the seething crowds who are just as excited as she is to meet their relatives.

At last she has broken free and rushes to him, embracing him with such feeling that it seems he is being caught in a vice. They speak in a mixture of English and German in loving terms before Frank takes her to his car. There is quite a long journey in front of them which is spent in excited chatter. He explains to her that his parents aren't with him as he wants her to be a surprise for them. He has told them that he is meeting an ex-airman friend who is coming to visit New York.

"Do you mean to say that they don't know about me? This may be difficult for all of us."

"No, I know them well enough to be able to say they will just love you after the initial shock. I know that they are a little old-fashioned and conservative and will probably be uneasy if we share the same bed. When they find out we are going to be married, they will probably change their thinking."

"I can understand them. My parents would be exactly the same, except I'm not sure they would accept such exciting, sleeping arrangements until we were actually married."

The journey soon passes as they have so much to talk about. Quite naturally, Frank's parents are amazed when this lovely girl arrives on the doorstep with a pile of luggage. Unlike Germany there is no formality regarding first names and she is introduced to David and Pat. There is initial reserve in their conversation, but soon they are all at ease until the question of marriage is brought up. The parents think it a little premature, but are staggered to find out that they have been in love for over six years and intend to be wed as soon as possible. They wonder if this is the same girl whose post Frank used to wait for impatiently all those years ago. When they both say "Yes" simultaneously, the parents realise that they are so obviously meant for each other, which causes Frank's mother to take her husband to an adjoining room. She returns to say that they have been discussing the matter and have decided that they can share a room — as she puts it. However, they are not to let anybody else know, especially their grandparents.

The couple are very contented with a bright future to look forward to. Helga is feeling that she is already at home as one of the family. She has applied to the state university and is awaiting a reply. Frank has quickly settled down at work in a job he feels very happy about. After all their trials and tribulations, all is turning out well. The wedding has already been arranged for January 20th. 1946.

All is not over yet, however, as Helga is experiencing some difficulties in gaining entrance to Frank's old university. It is not as easy as he had thought. She goes for interviews which are friendly enough, but of course she is competing with a great number of returning servicemen whose academic careers have been interrupted, or with those who want to start one. It is difficult if the university authorities were to allow a German to be a student in 1945 if they were having to turn down ex-servicemen. She is granted an interview when she is asked some searching questions about her work in the Law Faculty in Hamburg and her subsequent studies in Bremen which Helga answers confidently. After an interview of some thirty minutes or so, Professor Paul Johnston, a middle-aged reddish-haired man with spectacles perched on the end of his nose and close-set eyes, announced his decision and then gave her some advice and an offer to help her.

"Well, Fräulein Wassermann, I am rather impressed with your personality and knowledge of the subject. I have no hesitation in saying that I would in normal circumstances be delighted to have you as a student with your previous studies being taken into account. You were obviously very keen and committed to carry on your studies in Bremen when you quite understandably found it far too difficult to carry on at Hamburg. Your rapid promotion as a nurse indicates your intelligence and appreciation of your civic duties. However, these are not normal times and to turn down ex-servicemen in your favour would not be a good political move for us. The fact that you are German has no significance for me as I do not see you at all as a supporter of Nazi views or anyone we need to be wary of. You are a young lady of personality and intelligence who would be a credit to us I'm sure."

At this point Helga says how disappointed she is, but is grateful for his kind words.

"Just a minute young lady, I haven't finished yet. I could get you a position in an attorney's office where you could pick up experience which could stand you in good stead for a further application next year. Now this is what I am proposing to you. There is a fairly new college in a district of NY called Hempstead. It is called Hofstra and is like an offshoot of NYU, that is the University of New York. Now, I am very friendly with the admissions tutor there and I am sure we can do something between us. As I say, they are fairly newish and I think that they would welcome people like you. Already they are starting to get a good reputation."

"That is very kind of you, sir. Do you mind if I discuss it first with my future husband. "As she said these last few words she felt the thrill of being able to say this. She didn't go on to give more details of Frank as this could have been embarrassing for her, given his war record.

When she returns home she gives details of her afternoon with the professor who had been so understanding and helpful to her. They all agree that what he has proposed sounds a very acceptable alternative to going to Frank's alma mater, even if it doesn't carry quite the same reputation. The decision is made and the following day she calls the professor to say that she has taken up his advice to apply to this new college.

She arranges to meet the admissions tutor later in the week to discuss what he could offer to her. When she phones to confirm the appointment she is told that the man she needs to see is ill and the person answering the phone knows nothing about the offer. However, when he knows what she wants, he says he can put her onto somebody in the law department. This is done and the lecturer invites her to come and see him and discuss what they can do over coffee. She arrives at the university very smartly dressed, looking exceedingly pretty. She is shown to the office of a Dr Hinchliffe. He is a man with sandy-coloured, receding hair in a comb-over style, about in his mid-fifties and wears very thick glasses. The way he greets her puts her off as he leers at her and comes rather too close for comfort, especially as his breath is rather unhygienic. He seems more interested in her social life than he is in her knowledge of law and barely touches on her two years of study at Hamburg University. He says he finds her German accent very sensual and cannot take his eyes off her cleavage. Helga is very uneasy, gets up, makes her apologies before leaving the room, coffee untouched. Once in the street outside she bursts into tears.

29

ALL'S WELL THAT ENDS WELL

When Helga returns home, only Frank's mother is there to greet her. She tearfully tells her about her disturbing experience at the university.

"Did he think that because we have been defeated in the war and would be for ever considered inferior to our conquerors that he could behave like this? We barely touched on law, my qualifications so far, my views on various matters; no, all I could sense was that he was only looking at me as some feminine object, some decoration for the lecture room. Am I perhaps being conceited and all this is merely my imagination?"

"Well, my dear, you are certainly very attractive, but I understand how uneasy you must have felt. I wonder if this Dr. er . . . . Hinchliffe, did you call him, has a record of such behaviour? So you never even got round to discussing possible admission there?"

"No, Pat, I told him that I didn't feel very well, apologised, and left the room."

"Well, you did right. That is disgusting. We must ask Dave and Frank where we go from here when they get home."

Frank arrives home first to find a serious-looking mother and a very upset Helga. He is naturally very concerned and eventually manages to hear the story. His first reaction, recalling his character as a teenager, is to lose his temper as he threatens to go to Hempstead and sort out this unsavoury character who has so upset his girlfriend. His mother advises him, as she so often has in the past, to wait for his father before rushing into anything; he will know best. Dave comes home after what seems like an interminably long hour later to see a very upset family.

"What's wrong with you guys? Nobody's died, have they?"

He expresses disbelief when the story comes out and says that first thing next morning, whether the professor is ill or not, he will contact him with this news. The evening passes slowly, with nobody saying too much. They all having a sleepless night wondering where to go from here as far as Helga's future is concerned. She could get a job where her language skills would be appreciated or serve in a department store, but these alternatives are not what she really wants; her ambition is to be an attorney.

The family gets up the next day with Dave promising to ring his university friend as soon as possible. He and Frank leave for work just before 8 o'clock. They haven't been gone too long before the mail arrives. There are the usual bills and official-looking letters, before right at the bottom of the pile there is a letter addressed to Helga bearing the logo of The University of Pennsylvania. She opens it, reads it twice, three times, before throwing her arms into the air and shrieking in delight.

"What is this, Helga? What does this letter say?"

"I'm not sure whether this is a dream, but this is from Professor Paul Johnston who says that two candidates who had been offered places have dropped out, and asks if I would I like to accept one of the places. Would I! He said that he had been impressed with me, and besides they were short of women in the faculty. Hmm, I'm not too sure what that means that after my recent experience."

"Don't be silly, my dear, he is a highly respected senior professor, a real gentleman."

"Yes, I know, I was only joking. He seemed everything you say. I can't wait to tell Frank and Dave."

"Why don't you phone them now?"

This she does and Dave says this is good news and as an added bonus it will save him from having to make a 'phone call! Frank says he can't wait to come home.

All is fine now in the family, except for one thing. The following day on the Saturday Frank has to confess that he hasn't been sleeping too well as he keeps having nightmares in which he sees men parachuting, wings and engines flying past, B-17s hurtling to the ground, friends killed or maimed; he hears the sound of the engines as they are taxiing on the runway, their increased tempo as they take off and worst of all the coughing, spluttering sound of them as a wounded bomber limps its way home to the airfield. He is unwilling to go for counselling; what can he do with his wedding fast approaching?

Frank's father has told him that he ought to write a book about his experiences. This he says could act as some kind of purge of all these dreadful memories. There is a precedent as a First World War English soldier who had fought in the trenches did so and found it gave him some relief to get it out of his system. He says he will think about it.

A week or two later he tells his father that he has thought about it. He believes it is his duty and feels that he owes it to all those wonderful men he has served with to try and point out to the American people what they all went through so uncomplainingly to fight for what they believed in, even though many such as himself found their task in some ways against their better feelings.

What was it that made these men so special? Their average number of missions before death, serious injury or becoming a prisoner-of-war took them out of the firing line was a mere fifteen out of the twenty-five originally allowed before being withdrawn from flying duties. Most of them went on because they had great pride in the Eighth Air Force and in their group, there was a very strong esprit de corps. Most of them felt that they were invincible and it was other men who would be killed. They were all volunteers and could have asked to be transferred to other duties, but their belief in what they were doing prevented the majority of them from doing so. The motive for many of them for volunteering had perhaps been to avoid being drafted into the army or marine corps; it was considered preferable to lying in a foxhole or in a steamy jungle, surrounded by mosquitoes. In the USAAF if you survived a mission, you did at least have a comfortable bed to go to, and could eat proper food before going out in the evening. This was no consolation though if you saw your buddies with their faces and arms severely burnt or bodies shattered in pieces in a fuselage reeking of cordite.

These were the thoughts going through Frank's mind as he decided to write about his experiences and he would not spare criticism where he felt it was due, no matter who the people responsible were. He had a duty to tell it how it was. He sees himself as their spokesman, their story must never be forgotten and he has already decided on a title: "THE RELUCTANT WARRIOR."